This b

MISS GHOST

BOOKS BY RUTH M. ARTHUR

Dragon Summer

My Daughter Nicola

A Candle in Her Room

Requiem for a Princess

Portrait of Margarita

The Whistling Boy

The Saracen Lamp

The Little Dark Thorn

The Autumn People

After Candlemas

On the Wasteland

An Old Magic

Miss Ghost

Ruth M. Arthur

MISS GHOST

VICTOR GOLLANCZ LTD
LONDON · 1979

Copyright © 1979 by the Estate of Ruth M. Huggins

ISBN 0 575 02651 0

Printed in Great Britain by
St. Edmundsbury Press Limited
Bury St. Edmunds, Suffolk

For Briony, with love

Part One

Chapter One

I have never been quite sure whether parts of this story ever happened . . . was there really a Miss Ghost? Although I remember her with affection, and she lingers in my mind with sweetness, did I ever meet her, or was she only a fantasy of my imagination?

I shall never know for certain, though I owed her so much. The rest of my story is real, is true, however odd it may seem to me now—but I *am* rather an odd person, and this is a very strange story.

I think I always felt I was odd, unlucky, even when I was quite small for I remember once asking my father, "Why am I different from other children. Why?"

"You're not really different, pet, just . . . slower to make friends, more aloof, more self-contained perhaps, —but there's nothing *wrong* with you."

"Then why does Mother not love me?" I demanded.

That was a difficult one for even my father to answer, and he took his time over it.

At last he said rather sadly, "Your mother wanted a son; she had set her heart on having a boy when you were born."

"But, now that she's got Edward she still doesn't love *me!*" I pointed out.

"Never mind, pet, *I* love you, you know that," said my father comfortingly.

"Yes, I know," I said snuggling up to him, but I was not convinced about myself. I knew that people did not like me.

Later, I felt this difference in myself more acutely, for by then I stood alone in a cold, bleak world, a world without parents, without a home of my own, without love, a pitiless world—*my* world.

Yet once, I had a home, a father and mother like everyone else, a little brother, and a grandmother—Grannie Gilchrist.

I was happy then and cared for, sheltered and safe, a child like any other child—Elspeth Harrier of High Stair Rigg, Brockdale, Cumbria . . . but that was a long time ago.

Our house was old and white-washed, with a green door. It stood by itself a little way out of the village.

Behind it the high stair that gave it its name—giant steps of natural rock—mounted up the hillside towards the sky. Before it lay the black water of the tarn, fringed with reeds, where shy moorhens played hide and seek with Mrs. Pepper's ducks. Mrs. Pepper was our nearest neighbor.

The far end of the tarn was ringed with water lilies. pink and white, like a necklace, and beyond it lay the marsh where a heron lived and curlews called plaintively to one another.

I wasn't supposed to go near the marsh; there was no safe path across it and there were stories of people sinking into its dangerous bog and disappearing forever. But sometimes I could not resist the awful thrill of venturing a little way across it, jumping from tuft to tuft, avoiding the squelching mud, till, my excitement appeased, I returned safely to firm ground.

Edward, my brother, was only three when I first went to school in the village and I had to leave him at home. I didn't care for the other children, and they didn't like me—Edward was my only friend. I pretended that he was with me as I walked alone down the grassy track to the village past old Mrs. Pepper's house, and I talked and joked with him as if he was really by my side.

Sometimes on Sundays, for a treat, my father took me fishing, up the High Stair and across the fells to a little secret pool fed by a waterfall. There, while he fished, I played with Bella, the farm collie, who often accompanied us, or I hunted for frogs at the water's edge or sailed boats of twig over the waterfall till it was time to eat our sandwiches. Father and I alone together—*that* was happiness.

My father was a teacher and taught in the big school in the town down the valley, where I hoped to go when I was older. He was a quiet man and didn't talk much even to me, but he was full of knowledge.

Sometimes he got moody and depressed, shut up inside himself so that I could not get near him, but that darkness soon passed and he was himself again.

In the summer holidays we usually went up to Scotland for a week or two, Edward, Mother and I, to stay with her mother, Grannie Gilchrist—we called her Grannie Gil and I loved her best next to Father and Edward.

5

But suddenly everything began to change—or perhaps I became more noticing.

A coldness grew up between Father and Mother, and sometimes when I got in from school the house was empty, Mother and Edward absent, and I'd go along to Mrs. Pepper's house and peep through the hole in her door where the knot of wood had come out. If I could see her rocking in her chair by the fire, I'd knock and go in and stay beside her till Mother and Edward came home.

Father got very angry when he found out about this, and he and Mother shouted at each other, and their quarreling voices kept me awake at night. She went away oftener and took Edward with her, until one day when I got home from school they were gone, the house was silent and empty. They never came home again.

Father got into a frightful state when he came home and read the letter Mother had left. At first he hoped they'd come back any day, and we managed quite well on our own, but as time went on another letter came from Mother. She was going to marry again and go to Australia and she wanted a divorce. I heard Father telling Mrs. Pepper.

Something strange and terrible began to happen to Father after that, he went into one of his black moods, he didn't speak to me, and he didn't bother to get proper food. Often I used to hear him pacing up and down, up and down in the night, and sometimes crying. I couldn't bear to see him so desolate and unhappy but I didn't know how to comfort him.

I worried that he'd have to give up his teaching if he got any worse, but perhaps he was happier at school for

6

he loved his work, and there he could forget that Mother and Edward had gone.

When the summer holidays came, I was sure he'd get better, but he didn't, he got worse. Sometimes on the finest days he'd shut himself into his room and I could not coax him out to go for a picnic on our bicycles or over the fells to our fishing pool.

There was nothing nice to eat, just tinned food, and the house began to look dirty and neglected; even our clothes needed better washing than he gave them or than I could manage.

It was lonely for me too, with Father so silent and aloof, and I used to spend a lot of time in Mrs. Pepper's house, helping her to bake her scones and biscuits and cakes. She had put up a "TEAS" notice on her wall to attract walkers and to make a little extra money.

Sometimes she asked me questions about how we were managing at home, but I didn't tell her much; I didn't want her coming to our house in case she upset Father, and I was ashamed of its neglected state.

Then one day Father wouldn't get out of bed nor get dressed and I was frightened and ran to Mrs. Pepper and out came everything that I hadn't meant to tell her.

Mrs. Pepper comforted me and left me in her rocking chair with the cat while she went to see Father herself.

When she came back her face was flushed and worried.

"We'll have to get the doctor," she said. "Come you with me to the village, lambie, and we'll telephone."

She put on her good black coat over her apron and her hat instead of the man's cap she always wore at home; then she struggled into her shoes, kicking off her comfortable felt slippers, and we hurried down to the village.

She left me with Miss Black, my teacher, and later I saw the doctor's car and then an ambulance going up the track to our house.

"They're taking your father into hospital where he'll be taken care of," Miss Black told me, "and you'll stay here with me, dear, for a day or two, till you go up to your Grannie in Scotland."

After I had gone to bed I lay thinking over what had happened—it was like a nightmare. I felt terribly alone. Who would answer my questions about my father and about what was to happen to me if he had to stay in hospital for a long time? A confusion of thoughts and anxieties churned round in my mind, but then I remembered with relief that I was to go to stay with Grannie Gil. *She* would straighten everything out for me, I had great faith in her, and comforted I fell asleep.

Chapter Two

Grannie Gil lived in a house much too big for her, so that half the rooms were shut up; but she wouldn't move to something smaller. It was a rented house, it did not belong to her.

Maggie-Jean came up from the village every day to clean the house and cook and to look after Grannie.

Maggie-Jean wasn't very bright, a bit simple really, but she made the best treacle scones in the world, and often she let me help her in the kitchen.

It took nearly a whole day on the train to reach Grannie; it seemed a very long way from home to Scotland. I had some comics to read, and a box of sandwiches and potato crisps to eat, and a bottle of milk to drink; my suitcase was on the rack above me. I had only brought my immediate necessities, the rest were to be sent on by Mrs. Pepper later.

I thought about Mrs. Pepper while I gazed out of the window of the train at the fields and animals and houses flying past us. I liked Mrs. Pepper, she was old and comfortable to be with, she didn't nag or bother me, and she was always kind.

"You'll be back, lambie," she said as she hugged me goodbye at the station. "Be a good lass now."

She had found a corner seat for me and asked a woman already in the carriage to keep an eye on me, and I settled down to the long journey.

I must have fallen asleep after a while and was wakened by the woman opposite tapping me on the knee. "We'll be coming to your station in about ten minutes," she said. "I'll help you out with your case."

The Scottish air smelled fresher, crisper. I sniffed appreciatively. It would be nice to be staying with Grannie Gil again, whatever the reason.

She was there on the platform waiting for me, in her dowdy old jacket and her felt hat with fishing flies in bright colors hooked into its band.

I dropped my case on the platform and ran into her outstretched arms.

"Eh dearie!" she cried. "It's grand to see you again! And how you've grown! Come away now, Maggie-Jean's got a fine supper waiting for you."

Old Dougal the porter had already carried my case out to the waiting car.

"Thanks, Dougal. You'll remember my granddaughter Elspeth?"

"Aye, aye, I remember her fine," and Dougal. "Takes after yersel', Mistress Gilchrist. Have a care now," he added shutting the door carefully behind me.

Grannie Gil climbed into the driver's seat and after a series of snorts and backfirings the car lurched off, protesting. We hiccuped our way up the hills, and romped down them. Grannie drove most unevenly, but her house wasn't too far from the station, and soon, narrowly missing the gatepost, we shuddered to a halt at the front door.

Maggie-Jean came fluttering down the steps at once and folded me in a tight embrace the moment I got out of the car.

"So y're here, hen!" she squealed. "I never thought she'd bring you back safely!"

"Away in with her case, woman," snapped Grannie, "and less of your havering!"

Maggie-Jean made a face at me and stumped off with the case.

"I don't know why I put up with her!" Grannie grumbled. "She makes me so cross! —never mind she's devoted, you know, devoted."

I was given the little bedroom next to Grannie's, it was all white as fresh snow and on the windowsill stood a vase of great tawny-headed chrysanthemums, a blaze of color in the room.

On earlier visits I had shared a bigger room with Edward, and for a moment the thought of my little brother caught at my heart. I knew I would always miss him however long we were apart.

I got unpacked and tidied my things away, then I sat down by the window for a minute. The hills were nearer and not so big as I remembered them, beautiful in their autumn cloak of fading heather. There were sheep in the field next to Grannie's house, their bleating was a sound I loved, comfortable and reassuring.

There was a basin in my room so I washed my face and hands carefully to remove the grime of the journey, gave my hair a good brushing and went downstairs.

There was a lovely wood fire burning in the sitting

room, and Grannie Gil was drawing the curtains as I entered the room.

"That's right, dearie," she said looking me over approvingly. "I expect you'll be hungry; we'll have supper straightaway." I was glad to see that the table was set for supper cosily near the fire, instead of in the chilly and more formal dining room.

"I only use the one room now," Grannie explained. "It saves fuel, my bills are terrible. Go and tell Maggie-Jean we're ready, will you?"

I skipped into the kitchen where Maggie-Jean was putting the finishing scatter of parsley in the soup.

"We're ready, Grannie says. Can I carry anything for you?"

"Thanks, hen, take the milk jug in for me."

I picked up the jug carefully so as not to spill it, and Maggie-Jean bustled after me with the steaming soup in a tureen.

Bread and cheese were on the table, and a comb of honey from Grannie's bees, a bowl of apples and pears from the garden—and a plate of wonderful-looking treacle scones!

"Oh! yummy!" I breathed eyeing them.

"Och, I ken well they're your favorite," Maggie-Jean cackled, patting my shoulder. "Now see you get plenty to eat, hen. The fish pie's in the oven, M'm," she added turning to Grannie, "so I'll be off now. See you in the morn, hen, good night. And good night to you, M'm." She tripped out of the room, banging the tray on the door handle and making Grannie wince and sigh, "God give me patience, she's a sore trial." But the soup was fit for a queen, and the fish pie that followed so good that I had to have three helpings.

Grannie talked of this and of that but she didn't ask me the questions I dreaded. I noticed an air letter from Australia in Mother's writing propped up on the mantelpiece. She had not written to me since she left with Edward.

When we had finished supper and cleared the dishes into neat piles by the kitchen sink, I offered to wash up.

"Maggie-Jean will do it in the morning," said Grannie, "she'd never forgive me for driving you to it now!"

I laughed at Grannie's wry face; it was just what Maggie-Jean would have implied. It always amazed me the byplay that went on between those two as if they were sworn enemies, while everyone in the countryside knew they were utterly devoted to one another.

Later there was a short TV program, but soon I began to yawn, and Grannie sent me off to bed.

"Take a bath if you want to, and I'll be up soon to tuck you into bed," she said.

I was too tired to bother with a bath, in fact I had a struggle to keep awake till Grannie came up to say good night.

She opened the curtains so that I could see the stars, then she took my face between her hands and kissed me lovingly.

"Good night, my dearie," she said, "sleep well. It's lovely to have you here with me."

"Grannie . . . can I live here with you . . . always?" I asked hesitatingly. "You won't send me to . . . her in Australia?"

"I'll never do that," she promised. "This is your home now, and here you'll bide as long as I'm alive!"

Comforted, I fell asleep with her words echoing in my mind "Here you'll bide as long as I'm alive . . . alive . . . alive."

Chapter Three

After a day or two I felt perfectly at home in Grannie Gil's house and was happy to settle down to living with her permanently. She wasn't strict except when she had to be, and Maggie-Jean was always at hand to spoil me with luscious tidbits, it's a wonder I didn't become grossly fat.

At the village school I was looked over and accepted, no one bothered me. Nobody commented on my coming to live with my grandmother, no one asked me why. Evidently my story was not known and this made it easier for me to settle.

Grannie's house helped me too, for although Edward and I had stayed there with Mother, Father had never come with us, he and Grannie Gil did not get on very well. So the house held no painful associations with him for me, my only memories were of Mother and I didn't care about her, though I wished she hadn't taken Edward with her—he and my father were the ones who mattered to me.

One morning there was an official-looking letter on Grannie's breakfast plate and as she read it her face became very grave and she began to fidget as if she was nervous. At last she said straight out, "This letter is from the hospital about your father, dearie, you know he's . . . very ill?"

I nodded. "Is he ever going to get better?" I asked.

"Oh yes, indeed I hope so, but it may take a long time to get him well again," said Grannie with a grave face.

"It's a *mental* hospital he's in," I remarked, "that's for *mad* people, isn't it? Is my father mad?"

"He's mentally ill, sick in his mind, dearie, and he needs to be taken care of in hospital till he's better. They'll look after him well, you mustn't worry about him."

"Is his illness a catching thing, like measles or whooping cough?" I asked. "Is it something he could pass on . . . to anybody?"

"No, no, certainly *not*," Grannie exploded, "whoever suggested such a thing!"

"No one," I murmured, "I just wondered. Sometimes I worry about it. Shall I ever see him in hospital?" I asked half-fearfully.

"Later on perhaps," said Grannie, "you'll be able to visit him."

I sighed. I didn't want to see the sad stranger my father had become, I wanted to remember him as he used to be. I wanted to go on loving him.

I liked the school in Grannie's village. I enjoyed the orderliness of the classroom, and our teacher made the lessons quite exciting. The class was mixed and not too big, but although I got on quite well with everyone, no one seemed keen to make a special friend of me.

Chapter Three

"It's maybe your Englishness, hen; you speak different," Maggie-Jean commented when I told her.

"Give them time to get used to you," Grannie advised me.

Not that I minded much about friends, not at first anyway, for Edward continued to be my unseen companion for quite some time after he had gone. But as time went on his image dimmed until he became like a faint photograph of himself.

This may have been the reason why I turned my attention to a boy in my class who interested me, Neil Croft, a lame boy somewhat smaller than me. We spent our time together quarreling, taunting and goading one another, offering insults and jibes, sharpening our wits on one another, but all without rancor for we did not care enough about one another to wound.

In a strange way he was companionable, and gradually I came to respect and like him. He was a passionate observer of wild life—birds, beasts, insects—he knew a surprising amount about them for a boy of his age. My interest was aroused by him and I began myself to notice and observe the wild creatures of wood and moor and garden. Soon I had a thrush that ate from my hand and a red squirrel that came at my call.

But there was a large black cat belonging to Grannie's neighbor who was my enemy. When he stalked into the garden I drove him away, raging at him for scaring my birds. Once I saw him pounce on a young fledgling before I could stop him, and in a fury I rushed out cursing him, wishing him dead. He ran down the path, shot suddenly across the road right under the wheels of a passing car, and was killed instantly. I was shocked, horrified! Much as I hated that cat I had not seriously meant to damage him, and an uncomfortable feeling of guilt stayed with me for days. I felt that I was to blame for wishing him ill, and I found the whole episode very frightening.

Chapter Four

I enjoyed living with Grannie Gil. She was a real character, not just a dear old lady. We had some good times together, and I loved the excitement of outings in her car, for she drove like the wind, roaring round the corners, tearing down the hills, and urging the snorting machine up the steep slopes as one would a horse. A year passed and I had begun to feel safe, established and secure in a place of my own. The nightmare of Father's illness had receded—I hardly ever thought of Mother—and Grannie filled the place of my parents so well that I began to feel almost happy—Grannie Gil was enough for me.

When the summer holidays were approaching, a surprise letter came for me. It was from Mrs. Pepper, an invitation to come to stay with her for two weeks in August.

"Do you want to go, pet?" Grannie asked. "Who is Mrs. Pepper now? Have I heard of her? Miss Black, your teacher at Brockdale I know, for it was she who wrote to me when your Father took ill—but Mrs. Pepper?"

So I explained to her that Mrs. Pepper was our old friend and neighbor, our only close neighbor at High Stair.

"She's older than you, Grannie," I said, "and she can't get around a lot, her legs bother her, but I know her very well and she's always kind to me. I like her cottage too, which is nearer the tarn than ours. Yes, I'd like to go on a visit to her, please."

"Two weeks is quite a long stay if she's old," Grannie said thoughtfully. "Will you be all right?"

"Oh yes!" I cried unhesitatingly, "and I'll help her so she won't get too tired."

"Very well," said Grannie Gil. "Write and say you'll come, and I'll send Miss Black a little letter and tell her."

It was all arranged that I should go to Mrs. Pepper's for the first two weeks of August. We bought a new shirt to take with me, and I found a splendid pair of red canvas shoes, much to Grannie's delight though they didn't have any in her size.

"Shall I go to see Father?" I asked with a certain feeling of dread.

"Miss Black will find out from the hospital if he's well enough to see you and could take you over there," said Grannie. "Would you like to visit him?"

For a moment I hesitated. What would he be like, aloof, cold and grim-faced as he had become, a stranger who looked right through me as if I weren't there? Would he even know me?

My courage failed me, and I turned to Grannie.

"No, I don't want to see him," I said.

"Very well then, we'll wait till you're a bit older,"

said Grannie. "I'll write a note for you to give to Miss Black."

Grannie put me on the train next day with a good supply of Maggie-Jean's sausage rolls, a bottle of Coke, some potato crisps, an apple or two and a packet of sweets.

At the other end Miss Black met me at the station in a fine new Mini. She gave me a great hug. "That's my girl!" she exclaimed. "You haven't changed a bit, only grown taller."

She stowed my case on the back seat and drove carefully out of the station yard and along the road toward our village. She was a much better driver than Grannie Gil, and she concentrated more on the road so we didn't talk much. Soon we were through Brockdale and began to climb the hill to High Stair and Mrs. Pepper's house.

She tooted and Mrs. Pepper came out to meet us. "So here you are, lambie," she said kissing me warmly. "Eh, but it's good to see you again! Looks bonny, don't she, Miss Black?" she continued approvingly. "Come along in then, both of you, there's a cup of tea waiting."

She hobbled into her cottage and Miss Black carried my case, while I lingered for a moment to take a long appreciative look at the tarn, and then to cast a hasty glance at my old home looking so desolate and sad.

While we had our tea and tucked into Mrs. Pepper's good scones and shortbread, the latest news of the village was exchanged between Miss Black and Mrs. Pepper, but none of it meant much to me.

"Well, I'd better get back, I've work to do," said Miss Black jumping up after her third cup. "Come and see me at the schoolhouse, Elphie, any time you like," she said.

"Thank you, I will, and thanks for meeting me," I answered.

"So how's your Grannie?" asked Mrs. Pepper while I washed up the dishes. "And how's everything up there in Scotland? Have you settled down comfortable with her?"

"Oh *yes*," I assured her, "everything is just fine, but it's nice to be back here again too, with you, Mrs. Pepper."

"You'll do just what you like while you're here, lambie. There's a new pony across at Low Stile Farm, and they'll be glad of your help there with the hay-making. Your classmates are still around and you can ask some of them up here if you've a mind to."

I shook my head. "I'll maybe see them in the village," I said firmly. There was no one that I cared about.

"And you'll meet the new people across the way," continued Mrs. Pepper. "Tuffin their name is, and there's a girl, Goldie, about your age for you to play with."

I gave a gasp of surprise for it had never entered my head till then that of course our house must have been relet. I felt a burning resentment against the family who had taken it in our place, especially against the girl Goldie, before I had even met her! It was ridiculous to feel like this and I knew it, but my hostility was genuine and fierce.

Next morning I was on my way back from the village where I had done the shopping for Mrs. Pepper when I saw a girl walking up the path ahead of me. Goldie

Tuffin—what a silly name! She turned and saw me and waited for me to catch up with her.

"Hullo," she said in a syrupy voice. "You're the wonderful Elspeth Mrs. Pepper is always talking about. I know *all* about you."

Something patronizing in her tone infuriated me, and I'd like to have swept past her without a word, but obviously I couldn't. She was a pudgy girl with a pink and white face and big teeth that gave her mouth a greedy look. I saw at once why she was called Goldie, her mane of hair shone like spun gold; it was really gorgeous.

I wanted to say something spiteful to her but I couldn't think of anything nasty enough while she chattered on without a pause.

"We live in the house that used to be yours . . . it's not so nice as the one we came from, but Dad says it'll have to do in the meantime . . . of course we've altered it a bit inside to make it better."

I chose to ignore those remarks and hastened my pace so that she had a hard time keeping up with me, and I swore to myself that I would get back at her when I got the chance for what she had said about our home.

When we reached Mrs. Pepper's house, Goldie obviously hoped to be asked in, but I shot inside and shut the door firmly behind me.

Chapter Five

It was almost impossible to avoid so close a neighbor, and during the next few days Goldie hung about hoping to catch me as soon as I stepped outside.

But I was wily and left by the back door, where the path ran steeply down to the tarn, so that I escaped her. She wasn't really so bad, I suppose, and if she hadn't been living in *our* house I might have disliked her less, though her disparaging remarks about High Stair Rigg made me wild!

Once her mother invited me to tea, but I refused to set foot in the house and Mrs. Pepper had to make my excuses. Mrs. Pepper seemed to share my dislike of Goldie for she did not encourage her to come to her cottage as I had once done.

Mrs. Pepper's huge legs had grown worse in the year since I left High Stair and she found it difficult to get about at all, and but for the grocer's and butcher's boys who called twice a week I don't know how she'd have managed for food. She had even begun to talk of selling her cottage and moving down to the village; I was glad she had invited me to stay while she was still at High Stair.

I went up the High Stair, of course, climbing the rocks of the giant steps; I wandered across the fell to the little secret pool where my father used to take me fishing; but the pain of being without him in our special place and thinking how he had changed, distressed me so much that I sat down and cried on the rock where we used to picnic.

Once when I went down to the tarn to feed Mrs. Pepper's ducks, I wandered dreamily on along the path by the reeds that fringed it like eyelashes till I reached the far end where it disappeared into squelchy marsh. I looked across to the other side speculatively; it was only a few hundred yards across, a shortcut to the road that wound over the hill to the next valley. I thought of the gruesome stories I had heard of people disappearing in that little piece of bog, sucked down and swallowed up without a trace. I remembered with a shiver how I used to venture part of the way across it as long as my nerve held—could I still do it? I wondered idly.

My gaze wandered lazily over the landscape, the high fells, the valley, the tarn before me, Mrs. Pepper's house, and came to rest on my old home. It was then that I saw Goldie come out of the house and stand in the garden, shading her eyes with her hand as she scanned the scene—she was looking for me. When she spotted me, she waved and ran down the hill toward the tarn and the path I had followed.

I did not want her with me, distracting me with her incessant chatter. Somehow I had to escape from her, but where? On a sudden daft impulse I jumped up and began to flit across the treacherous bog. Miraculously my feet seemed to find their old way as I stepped from tuft to tuft, lightly and quickly, managing to avoid the evil pockets of mud. I dared not stop for a moment to think about the danger. I just skimmed on right across till I reached the other side safely. Then my knees gave way and I sank trembling onto the solid turf of the hillside.

Then, and only then, did I have time to look back, and to my horror saw that Goldie had reached the end of the tarn and was about to follow me across the bog.

"Go back! Go back!" I yelled. "It's dangerous! You'll sink right in over your head! Go back!" But she paid no attention to my cries and began to come across jumping from tuft to tuft as I had done, and she was heavier than I am.

A kind of panic took hold of me as I realized that I was helpless to stop her, and anger shook me at her stupidity in not taking my warning seriously.

"All right, sink then, and serves you right," I said aloud. Almost as I spoke her foot slipped and in a moment she was in a pocket and up to her knees in the evil mud, sinking rapidly.

I was horrified. I didn't know what to do! She was much too heavy for me to pull her out but something must be done at once to save her or it would be too late.

I opened my mouth and began to scream at the top of my voice. Luckily two young climbers with a rope who were passing near heard my cries for help and came to Goldie's rescue, though it took them some time to pull her out of the mud.

Chapter Five

I walked home with her, feeling a bit ashamed of myself, and Mrs. Tuffin nearly passed out when she saw her daughter.

"I fell in the mud, but I'm not hurt a bit," Goldie told her, and not another word about it did she say. I couldn't help admiring her for not making a thing of it, and evidently she didn't attach any blame to me—but I felt it was really my fault, and I did not dare to think how differently it could have ended.

Chapter Six

The two weeks of my visit passed quickly and it was not until the last few days that I began to long for home and Grannie Gil. I felt I no longer belonged at High Stair, my place had gone and I had sunk to the status of a visitor.

On my last afternoon I set off across the fells for our little pool, taking Bella with me for company—the dear collie had not forgotten me. I wanted to preserve in all its beauty a memory of that secret place in which Father and I had delighted. I hoped to recapture the magic we had shared.

The same heron flapped clumsily across the pool, the same curlews called plaintively to one another, but the magic was gone, and I only felt the more sharply what I had lost.

Would my father ever recover enough to come home again, back into my life? I felt that I did not know him any more, but I wanted to remember him as he used to be when I had loved him so dearly.

There was a letter from Grannie Gil waiting for me when I got in, full of little tidbits of village gossip and complaints about Maggie-Jean. "Hurry home, pet," she wrote, "I'm missing you."

My father was not mentioned so there can't have been any news. I asked Mrs. Pepper if *she* ever heard anything about him.

"Nothing, lambie," she said shaking her head. "Poor man, it's a sad business, but maybe he'll recover in time. You must go on hoping."

On my last evening I went to supper at the schoolhouse with Miss Black.

"And Mrs. Pepper, Elphie?" she asked. "How do you find her?"

"I've liked being with her," I said slowly, "but she can't manage so well on her own now, her legs are so bad."

Miss Black nodded. "Just as I thought, she shouldn't be alone up there. She'll have to move down into the village and we'll all help her."

"She knows this," I said. "She talked of selling her house." I sighed.

"Nothing ever stays the same for long does it?" I said reflectively. "High Stair will be quite different when Mrs. Pepper has gone. I won't ever want to go back there again."

"I'm sorry, love," said Miss Black laying a gentle hand on my arm, "about your father, and . . . everything, it's been a hard time for you, but you're all right with your grannie, aren't you?"

"Oh *yes*," I replied cheering up immediately. "It's lovely living with her, so safe and settled; she's old and comfortable you see—and I can depend on her. It's the best home I could wish for."

Grannie's words suddenly echoed in my mind. "Here you'll bide as long as I'm alive."

"Then that's all right," said Miss Black. "I'm very glad. You must stay with me next time you come here."

I thanked her, but I knew I'd never come back.

I left next morning, and Miss Black put me on the train. All the way north my pleasure increased as the wheels of the train beat out in lively rhythm, "I'm going home again, home, *home*! I'm going home again, home, *home*!"

Grannie was waiting on the platform to meet me. I dropped my case and ran into her outstretched arms, where she stood steady as a rock, inviolate, unchanging.

"How are you, dearie? Oh, it's good to have you home again!" she cried. "Come on, then."

Old Dougal picked up my case and followed us out to the car.

"You'll be happy now the lassie's back, Mistress Gilchrist," he said shutting the door behind her. "Go carefully now. . . ." The rest of his words were drowned in the roar as Grannie drove off and I turned to wave goodbye to him.

Grannie Gil was at the top of her form, the car bucked and snorted, rushed and hesitated under her hand like a live thing, and it wasn't until we shot past the house that I realized the brakes weren't working properly.

Maggie-Jean was peering anxiously out of the front door when at last we arrived; we'd had to go two or three miles along the road to turn, and nearly got stuck in a ditch.

"I thought yez was never comin'!" she squealed, rushing out to wrench my door open and half lifting me out of the car. "What a time it's taken yez to get here! Come away in now, yer room is all ready for y'."

"Away and bring the supper in, woman," snapped Grannie. "I hope it's ready?"

"Ready and waitin' this hour back," panted Maggie-Jean fussing over my suitcase.

"Then it'll be too dried-up to eat!" was Grannie's parting shot. But I caught the nod and smile they exchanged behind my back as I turned to go into the house, they were both delighted to have me home again.

That night when Grannie came to tuck me into bed she brought me a little gold locket on a thin chain.

"I want you to have this Elphie," she said. "It's my lucky charm; you keep it," and she fastened it round my neck.

School started again and I moved up into the next class. I liked my new teacher, she had the knack of making even the duller lessons come alive. And I had a friend in Neil Croft. At last I began to feel secure enough to let some of my guard down, to open my shutters, to expect enjoyment, to accept friendship, and to look forward to a settled tomorrow with confidence. I grew fond of Grannie's house though she herself gave it little thought. Her care was all lavished on her garden, which she loved, and where she worked tirelessly, cursing her stiff knees as she knelt weeding her flower beds or bedding out new plants with careful loving hands. I loved the garden too, though I didn't often work in it. I liked to climb into an apple tree to read, or stretch out flat on my stomach in the shade to do my homework when the weather was fine enough.

On Saturdays I helped with the shopping, and when Maggie-Jean did her baking, I was usually on hand to sample her goodies and to pull faces of disgust to tease her.

On Sundays I put on my best clothes and accompanied Grannie to church; Maggie-Jean and almost everyone in the village was there. I liked the singing and the organ music, and although the solemnity of the service impressed me, the most important thing to me was that I felt myself to be a member of a community, taking my part in the ancient rituals of worship.

Then there were the cosy winter evenings, when Maggie-Jean had gone home, and Grannie and I drew the curtains to shut out the dark and settled down in the firelit room, she with her knitting, her sharp eyes peering over the top of her glasses at the TV program we had chosen to watch. Sometimes we listened to music on the radio, or I read aloud to Grannie till it was time for me to go up to bed. I was happy then, cherished and safe, encouraged to flourish and blossom like one of Grannie's plants.

But my trust came too soon. Early in January disaster struck, disaster so catastrophic that it finished everything for me.

Grannie Gil was killed in a car accident.

She must have spun off the road at a corner, and I was told the car turned over twice on its way down the side of the hill.

Grannie was hardly damaged visibly, the doctor said he thought she must have died before the car reached the bottom of the slope. No one knew *how* it had happened, only that it was all over for her, finished.

Chapter Six

It was the very worst thing that could have happened to me. With Grannie Gil gone it was the end of my world.

I was too much shocked to grieve for her; that came later. My main concern was what was to happen to me? Who would care for me now? Where was I to live? I developed a bad stammer and couldn't get my words out, it was horrible and increased my confusion.

Everyone was very kind to me. Neil Croft's mother took me in to look after me till some arangement could be made for me. Neil, in unspoken sympathy, gave me part of his precious birds' egg collection. Maggie-Jean collapsed completely and had to be taken into hospital.

Miss Jenner, a friend of Grannie's who was a social worker and whom I knew slightly, came to talk to me about my future; but the only thing I could be absolutely certain about was that nothing would persuade me to go to Mother in Australia. I repeated over and over again, "I *won't* go, so don't try to send me. I won't go, I'd rather *die!*"

Miss Jenner had the sense to see that I really meant it. "We'll have to find foster parents for you," she said, "kind people who will take you into their home and treat you like one of their own children."

I nodded unenthusiastically. I was prepared to accept anything so long as it was not being sent to Australia.

In the end Miss Jenner herself took me in for a couple of weeks, and during this time we went by car to a village about fifteen miles away to see a family who wanted a foster child.

Their house was nice but dull, like a child's drawing, it had a garden and was near the village shops. Tucker was the name of the people. Mr. Tucker, who looked a little younger than my father, was an estate agent. He worked very hard and was away from home a good deal, so I did not see much of him.

Mrs. Tucker wore glasses and very high-heeled shoes. She had worked in a dress shop and liked to wear pretty clothes. "Ferret-face!" I thought to myself when I first saw her. I did not take to her nor she to me. Though she put on a welcoming manner for Miss Jenner's sake, I knew that it was false.

There were two children, Posy, a pudgy little girl several years my junior, and a darling baby, little Stew, a few months old.

They seemed nice enough people—"decent folk" Grannie would have called them—but they weren't very warm or friendly or interesting and on the way back Miss Jenner voiced some doubts about them.

"They're not quite the family I'd hoped to find for you, Elphie," she said, "and it's rather a peculiar village, old-fashioned and superstitious, but there's not much choice at the moment. What do you think? Did you like them? D'you think you'd be happy there?"

"I don't know," I said, "they seemed all right, the baby is lovely. I suppose. . . . I couldn't just go to boarding school, could I? Is there any money?"

Miss Jenner shook her head. "Not enough," she said. "I think you should give the Tuckers a try, you need a *home*, Elphie."

"All right," I agreed. "When?"

"Next week," Miss Jenner replied.

"Perhaps they won't want to take me?" I suggested hopefully.

34

"Mrs. Tucker said they'd have you before we left their house," Miss Jenner replied.

So that was it, and I moved in to live at "The Nook" with the Tuckers, bringing with me everything I possessed. I meant to make the best of it, and I thought that with little Stew to love, life needn't be too bad.

Chapter Seven

At first everything at the Tuckers seemed quite nice. I had a small bedroom of my own looking out over the garden to fields and woods and the sky; there was plenty to eat; I was warm and comfortable and encouraged to think of the Tuckers as "home"— but I had no sense of belonging.

Posy took a great liking to me and wanted me with her all the time, demanding my attention till I was fed up with her.

But the baby, little Stew, was adorable. I think I loved him at once and put him in Edward's place to be petted and doted on as my little brother had been.

I was slightly scared of him at first for I had never handled a young baby, but I soon learned how to manage him and took a big share in looking after him.

At first, as I said, all went well, but after a month or two the smiling surface of life at "The Nook" began to crack. Mrs. Tucker worked so hard at being *nice* to me that I knew she had no more real liking for me than I had for her. Of Mr. Tucker I saw very little, his work took up most of his time.

Chapter Seven

Posy grew jealous of my affection for the baby and withdrew her approval of me. I soon discovered her to be a dreadful little liar and tale-teller, and often I was blamed for her misdeeds.

At school my stammer was embarrassing, and the other children tended to avoid me. I soon found that having no parents or home of my own set me apart, I didn't quite fit in. I was not one of the herd. So my feeling of isolation, of oddness, increased, my sense of not belonging deepened.

Only with little Stew was I completely at ease; in loving and caring for him I was happy. And gradually I came to realize that as long as I made myself useful to Mrs. Tucker, as long as she could trust me to look after the baby, I would keep my place in the household.

So when Miss Jenner came to see how I was getting on I made no complaint, for little Stew made up to me for all the things I missed at the Tuckers, and I was content to stay with them because of him.

Posy's jealousy increased, and I had to be constantly on my guard for I was afraid that she might damage the baby and put the blame on me.

Once she took the brake off the stroller outside the shop I was in, and only the quick action of a passerby saved it from tipping off the pavement onto the road. She told her mother what had happened when we got back, and of course I was blamed for carelessness.

"Posy, you're telling lies again!" I cried. "It was *you* who took the brake off! You'll have to watch her," I said turning to Mrs. Tucker, "she's jealous of the baby and she'll harm him if she can!"

"Harm her own little brother? *Surely* not," said Mrs.

Tucker incredulously, giving me a suspicious look while Posy smiled triumphantly.

There were other incidents like this, though I think Mrs. Tucker cannot have believed all Posy's tales or she'd never have let me stay, no matter how useful she found me.

A year passed and I had settled into the Tucker household and had made a place for myself caring for little Stew, though I never could feel that it was "home."

Certain people in the village began to show some friendliness towards me when I was out with the children. Mr. Tweedie at the shop slipped many a toffee drop into my hand along with Mrs. Tucker's change, and when I went to the farm for eggs, past Miss Brock's cottage, I would stop ,and offer to fetch her eggs along with ours.

She and her brother lived alone, each of them so twisted with rheumatism that I wondered how they managed to cope at all.

Their cottage was full of odd corners and alcoves and cupboards where they kept their collections of china, of brasses, of butterflies, of shells and Miss Brock's jewelry —gewgaws her brother called them. She kept them all— brooches, pendants, earrings, bracelets, buckles— jumbled up in a large wooden box. "It's not *real* jewelry," Miss Brock told me, "but pretty, don't you think." Each piece had its own story.

Sometimes for a treat when I brought the eggs I was allowed to take out and admire her treasures, even to try them on myself before the mirror. My favorite piece was a silver pendant like a big snow crystal, which came from Finland, Miss Brock said. For a treat I was sometimes allowed to wear it while I was in their cottage. Like most old people Miss Brock was forgetful and confused at times, she would forget to pay me for her eggs or try to pay me twice, and she was always losing her glasses, or her purse, or the pills for her rheumatics.

One day I was caught by a thunderstorm and had to spend nearly an hour in the cottage before I could go back to the Tuckers. I asked to be allowed to wear the pendant while I helped Miss Brock to clean the silver. When the sky cleared at last, I put the pendant carefully back into the box before I said goodbye.

A few days later when I stopped on my way to the farm I found Miss Brock's back door locked. Usually I knocked, opened the door and called—it had never been locked before. So I knocked more loudly and waited and knocked again. After a minute or so the door was unlocked and Miss Brock stood there very straight and dignified with a stern face. "S-S-Shall I get. . . ." My words faltered and died before her look of hostility.

"Wh-wh-whatever is w-wr-wrong?" I asked gazing up at the stony face.

"You should know," she said coldly. "My silver pendant has gone—vanished."

"Your pendant . . . vanished?" I repeated foolishly, "b-but *when*, how?"

"You had it last," said Miss Brock accusingly, "and no one else ever touches it. What did you do with it, child?"

"I put it back in your box," I replied instantly,

"where I always put it!" Suddenly the awful implication dawned on me, she thought I had stolen her pendant, pinched it for myself! I was outraged!

"If you'll bring it back at once, we'll say no more about it," said Miss Brock.

"But *I* didn't take it!" I cried angrily. "How can you think such a thing of me!"

She stood looking at me suspiciously, accusingly, and I felt a blush beginning to spread all over my face, not of guilt but of shame at her low estimation of me.

"I'm very sorry you've lost it," I said quietly, "but it has nothing to do with me, I promise you."

"I don't believe you, but there is no more to be said," Miss Brock replied. "You are no longer welcome in this house. Good afternoon," and she shut the door in my face.

I was aghast, humiliated and bitterly hurt, but I decided it was wiser to say nothing to anyone and to hope that somehow the pendant would be found.

She must have dropped a hint, perhaps unintentionally, for a whispering campaign against me began in the village and once or twice "thief" was hissed at me as I passed along the street. I felt ostracized and guilty, although I was completely innocent. Eventually the gossip reached Mrs. Tucker's ears and she tackled me at once.

"What's this I hear about Miss Brock's silver pendant?" she asked accusingly. "They say you stole it!"

"Well, I *didn't* whatever *they* say!" I cried.

"I should hope not indeed. I don't want a thief under my roof, let me tell you. Are you quite sure you didn't take it?"

Chapter Seven

"Of course, I'm sure!" I shouted furiously but she did not seem convinced that I was telling the truth.

For nearly a month I lived under a shadow of suspicion. I got hostile looks from some people in the village, and I was ignored by others; I withdrew more and more into myself, hiding from accusing eyes. And something began to harden in me, some inner core of hurt and bitterness. Evidently human beings were not to be trusted; they turned against one. It was safer to be self-sufficient, to trust none of them, to keep apart from the crowd and count only on oneself.

Then one afternoon when I got in from school, Mrs. Tucker met me at the door as if she'd been looking out for me.

"Miss Brock wants to see you, she's waiting in the lounge," she whispered.

"What does the old bag want?" I asked rudely.

"Hush, Elspeth, what a way to speak!" said Mrs. Tucker shocked.

I tossed my head defiantly and marched into the sitting room, shutting the door behind me. Miss Brock who was sitting sedately upright rose to her feet as I came in and held out her hand. I saw that she was distressed for her hand was shaking and her lips trembled as she spoke.

"My dear child," she said, "I have come to apologize. My pendant has been found, and I don't know how to tell you how sorry I am to have blamed you for its loss."

I was greatly relieved to hear it but I remained stony-faced as I said, "I'm glad you've found it—you see I was telling you the truth when you called me a thief and a liar. Where was it found?"

"You'll never believe it," said Miss Brock confidentially. "I found it inside the hem of a dress I haven't worn for some time. Somehow it must have slipped down inside it—I'm afraid I have become very absent-minded for I don't even remember wearing the pendant since you last had it. It was wrong of me to accuse you of stealing it," she continued, "and to show you how sorry I am, I should like you to have it to keep," and she held it out to me.

I felt so embarrassed I did not know what to do. I never wanted to see the wretched thing again. But Miss Brock was insistent and quite determined, so I took the pendant from her hand and opening the door I called Mrs. Tucker. "Miss Brock wants me to have this pendant now," I explained. "She found it; you see, I didn't pinch it."

"How generous of you," Mrs. Tucker gushed turning to Miss Brock, "Elspeth will be proud to accept such a lovely gift, won't you, dear? I hope you have thanked Miss Brock nicely?"

"Thank you, Miss Brock," I said dutifully, and I stalked out of the room. In the attic I held the pendant in my hand for a moment, gazing down at its delicate beauty, but for me it had lost its appeal and I dropped it carelessly into a drawer among my handkerchiefs.

Mrs. Tucker soon spread the story around how Miss Brock had found the pendant and given it to me. But somehow a question was left in the air, the damage had been done, the facts were forgotten and people only remembered that there had been that queer story about Elspeth Harrier and a theft.

Then Posy got chicken pox, and we were all in

quarantine when Mrs. Tucker burned her arm on the electric stove. Luckily I was able to manage the extra work, to look after the baby, and to help to nurse Posy, and I didn't get chicken pox myself. As long as she was ill, I felt sorry for her and tried to please her with stories and attention, but once she was over the worst my dislike for her returned. She had lost a lot of weight while she was ill, which certainly improved her looks, but she didn't regain her strength and was wan and ailing throughout the summer.

There were a series of minor disasters in the house that summer: the hot water tank burst and did a lot of damage; lightning struck the chimney during a summer storm and it had to be rebuilt. Then Mr. Tucker's car was involved in an accident and had its side bashed in though he wasn't hurt. Little Stew was the only one of the family who was not affected and I loved him more than ever.

It was about this time that the whispering started up again, worse than ever.

"All this bad luck, these mishaps—what's causing them—or who?" one old crone was heard to mutter. "Stands to reason it must be *someone* in the village."

Chapter Eight

When the summer holidays started, I had a letter from Miss Black. She had hoped to invite me to stay with her, but her mother had taken ill and she would have to go and look after her, she said. It was disappointing, but Mrs. Tucker promised to take me to stay with Posy's grandmother at the seaside when they all went. But a few days before we were to go, a message came from the grannie that her beloved cat had died, and she was so upset that she hadn't the heart for any visitors—so the visit was off.

"It's very strange," Mrs. Tucker remarked when she read the letter, "how many things have gone wrong for us lately. We seem to have had more than our share of bad luck—since you came to live with us, Elspeth," she added pointedly.

I shrugged it off at the time, but the idea grew, it was not pleasant to be called a bringer of bad luck, and the more I thought about the disasters that had happened to the Tuckers, the more I came to believe that there might be some truth in her words.

Mrs. Tucker must have talked in the village for I met

Chapter Eight

a new wave of hostility, sidelong looks, suspicious
glances. Some people crossed the street so as to avoid
me—I'm sure I could not have imagined it all. It was
horrible and I was driven even further into myself;
without little Stew I don't know what I'd have done.
But I did have one compensation, one escape. I discovered the world of books and became an obsessive
reader. Once a week when the library van came round I
was first into it and jubilantly carried to the Tucker's
house an armful of volumes. I read mainly in bed at
night for Mrs. Tucker complained if she discovered me
with my nose buried in a book during the day. I read
widely and voraciously, anything, everything that I
could find, and wonderful new horizons opened up
before me.

This certainly helped for it gave me a way of escape,
but I still had to suffer the day-to-day living under a
cloud. I may have exaggerated in my mind the feeling
of the village's dislike, its ostracization of me, for I'm
sure most people were much too sensible to believe the
gossip that went round about me, but there were certain
old people, village characters, eccentrics who would believe any tale, and I think it was they who stirred the
pot and kept the gossip simmering. I hoped that when
the summer was over and the silence of winter shut
people into their houses, the nasty gossip would die
down.

Soon there was the nip of frost in the air, mornings
and evenings were crisp and clear, apples ripened and
mellowed, the berries of rowan and hawthorn and holly
were reddening for Christmas; the cuckoo had long
since gone and owls hooted eerily at dusk from the

woods. The swallows had flown from their nest outside my window, leaving me with a sense of desertion. Any day now I expected to see the threads of wild geese flying over to their winter quarters on the marsh; summer was gone, and winter's dark cloak dropped over the land.

Misfortunes continued to fall on the Tucker home. A window was blown in during a gale; a wall of the house began to crack and subside and had to be expensively underpinned. Finally, the central heating went wrong in the first cold spell and took a long time to put right while we all shivered.

Mrs. Tucker was thoroughly upset. "Whatever next?" she cried. "This has become a most unlucky house!"

The look she gave me was chilling, as if somehow she held me responsible for their troubles. I knew this was nonsense, of course, but it did not help my self-confidence.

Nor was that the end of the misfortunes that fell in an ever widening circle. Foot and mouth disease broke out on one of the farms in the district; and the farmer from whom we bought our eggs had several of his sheep worried by an unknown dog. Then the old man who came to collect our pig food fell down the steps into the garden and broke his arm; and the postman skidded off his bicycle outside the Tucker's house and cut his head so badly that he had to have nine stitches in it.

The whispering against me in the village grew and spread and grew, as each new disaster was laid at my door. "There's been a curse on this place," an old woman muttered, "ever since that girl came to the

Tuckers, mark my words." I was in the shop at the time, and I heard it said with so much certainty, that I was half convinced myself that in some unknown way I carried ill-luck around with me.

Then I noticed something new in the hostile looks that were given me, an element of fear—they were afraid of me as if they believed I had the power to damage and to harm. In a strange way this boosted my self-confidence and encouraged me to cultivate a tougher, more aggressive mask to conceal my real self.

There was a brisk young woman I rather liked, a friend and neighbor of Mrs. Tucker's, who turned up one day with a tale of woe. Her dog, out on a shoot with her husband, had been swept over a waterfall and drowned. She was very upset about it.

"One more disaster," remarked Mrs. Tucker lowering her voice and partly closing the door behind her as she took her friend into the sitting room to tell her the latest gossip.

"Well! Really!" exclaimed the girl a few moments later in a clearly angry tone. "No one can blame Elspeth this time! It's ridiculous, this talk in the village of the evil eye. What a load of rubbish! It ought to be stopped, it's not fair on the girl!"

Someone shut the door and I could not hear any more. The evil eye—what *did* she mean? There was no one I felt I could ask, but about a week later Mr. Tucker had to go into town on a Saturday morning and offered to take me with him.

It was the chance I had been hoping for to get to the library, so I jumped at it, and took a list of shopping for Mrs. Tucker with me. We had a very nice morning,

and Mr. Tucker took me to a cafe where we had coffee
and cakes and he talked to me as if I were a *person,* not
just an encumbrance. It was about the first time I'd ever
been alone with him, and I found myself liking him
much more than I'd thought I did.

I got the shopping done quickly and then found my
way to the library, it was only a small town with everything of importance in the main street. I soon got what
I wanted from an enormous dictionary. "Evil eye: A
look of ill will. The supposed faculty of injuring by a
look." *"Supposed"*—as I suspected, it was all nonsense
and superstitious ignorance! I came back to the Tuckers
almost ready to laugh at the absurdity of it all—evil
eye indeed!

All those disasters that had been attributed to me
were only unfortunate coincidences, dramatized by
some of the superstitious old folk in the village. I remembered Miss Jenner warning me of this before I
came to live with the Tuckers. And yet . . . the feeling that I was an unlucky person persisted, unlucky to
others, unlucky to myself. Why? Was there something
incomplete about me that made me unattractive, friend-
less, even unable to love? Perhaps if I could make one
real friend, one who cared deeply for me, one I could
trust and who trusted me, my luck might change, the
pattern of ill-fortune that seemed to have followed me
through most of my life could be broken, and I might
become a whole and loveable person.

But I was afraid to try. I did not dare lay myself
open to further rebuffs by making a friendly approach
to anyone, it seemed safer to encourage people to fear
me, to keep my isolation by making myself unattractive.

Chapter Nine

Then for a time things went better. I won a prize for my Christmas cake in cookery at school, which pleased Mrs. Tucker, and I began to develop quite an interest in cooking. Little Stew, now a sturdy toddler, was still my special pet, and Posy no longer gave me much trouble for she was afraid of me and had learned that it was as well to keep on my right side. I had gotten used to Mrs. Tucker, and although I didn't like her any better, we tolerated one another.

At school I did well enough, but I knew I could have done much better if I had liked my teacher, Miss Hunt, more. As it was, she seemed to take a delight in disparaging me as often as possible, perhaps she took my aloof manner for conceit. I suppose like most girls on entering their teens I was unpredictable, my moods as variable as an April day, good one day, bad the next. After taking a lot of trouble over one of my essays, I was disappointed and depressed when Miss Hunt returned it to me to do again.

She blew me up in front of the class, and I felt thoroughly humiliated and angry.

"Do it again, and try to use such brains as you have this time," she said.

I stood silent for a minute frowning across the class-room at her with what I hoped was a look of disdain, of scorn. There was a sudden stillness in the room as the class watched, holding its breath, then an audible sigh as I lowered my eyes and sat down in my place.

A few days later when Miss Hunt was giving two members of the class a lift home in her car, a lorry hit her at the crossroads and severely injured her shoulder.

The next morning school was agog with excitement, and I became aware of whispering groups breaking up hurriedly when I appeared, of scared glances exchanged, of eyes avoiding mine.

Sometimes at the end of the day Anna Strong and I used to walk home together, and on this particular day I waited at the school gate to see if she would join me. When she approached me, someone called out, "Don't go with her, Anna, it's not safe. Look what happened to Miss Hunt!"

Anna tossed her head and paid no attention, "Silly cows," she muttered as we swept through the gate to-gether and set off along the road. I was grateful for her company, but when we reached her house she turned her back on me and did not ask me in; our relationship went no further.

There were the usual mishaps and accidents in the school, the kinds there always are, and I knew that a section of the class liked to believe that I was respon-sible. The feeling against me grew so strong that I al-most began to believe in my own power. I found I could really scare the other children, frighten them into a kind of awe of me, and this delighted me for I felt I was getting some compensation for the loneliness and isolation I suffered.

As a gesture of defiance, I cropped my hair very short and uneven, and I must have looked quite repulsive for I shocked Mrs. Tucker. I wanted to repel and antagonize, and I think I succeeded.

Miss Jenner continued to take an interest in me, and she was good about visiting me fairly regularly. I could see that she was sometimes worried about me, for she must have seen a change in me, though I usually showed her my best side. When she questioned me about my life at the Tuckers, I did not answer entirely truthfully, for I hid my unhappiness from her, and when she suggested that I might like to move to another family, I reacted strongly. "I could not possibly leave little Stew," I cried, "he needs me and I need him. I *must* stay here."

About this time I asked Miss Jenner to write to the hospital to get the latest news about my father. It was still bad, his case was very complicated and there was no question of his leaving hospital.

It was Miss Jenner's idea that I should write to him sometimes. "It will keep you in touch with one another," she said. The letters I wrote were short and cheerful, pleasant accounts of little incidents about Stewart, or some outing I had had with the school, nothing that showed my loneliness or my heartache. But when no reply ever came I grew discouraged. Then I began to write longer letters, letters that gave a truer picture of my life. I poured out on paper my longings, my resentments, my hopes and my fears. Those letters were never sent. I found them a kind of safety valve, they gave me a certain relief. Also they made me think about my father, they established a fragile thread of contact between us.

When I had been living with the Tuckers for nearly two years, Miss Jenner came to tell me that my name would soon be coming up for adoption. Would I like to be adopted by the Tuckers if they suggested it, she asked me.

"I'll have to think about it," I told her.

It was very difficult for me. Theirs was the only home I had known since Grannie Gil died, and it was not so bad; school had its nasty side but another might be worse, and although I did not care for Mrs. Tucker or for Posy, I really loved little Stew, and for his sake I was willing to stay with the Tuckers and even to be adopted by them.

Stewart was a lively little boy and had reached the stage when he was mischievous and sometimes destructive. We were all careful to keep anything precious out of his reach, but every now and then he managed to get hold of something of Posy's—a doll or toy—and to break or damage it.

On Saturday mornings I went to work for old Mrs. McPhee, and with the money I earned plus some of my pocket money I bought a beautiful book of colored photos of animals—it was my pride and joy. Somehow Stewart got hold of it, and by the time I found him surrounded by torn pages, much of my book was destroyed.

"Stewart!" I yelled. "Oh Stew! How could you! You naughty, naughty boy!"

His face puckered up and he began to howl, so I picked him up and hugged him.

"Never mind," I wailed. "It's done now and I don't suppose you meant to hurt me, did you?"

Two days later Posy and Stewart were playing together in the garden when I notice that Stewart had disappeared and the door of the greenhouse—which was always kept bolted—was wide open. I tore outside calling his name, my voice wild with panic as I shot into the greenhouse.

He lay there, quite motionless, face downwards in the deep rainwater tank in the floor. "He's dead!" I gasped, "drowned. My little Stew . . . is drowned!"

Chapter Ten

He wasn't drowned, though it was a very close thing. My screams brought Mrs. Tucker running, and she sent Posy for Jean MacIntosh next door, while I rang the doctor. Jean was a nurse and luckily was at home, and by the time the doctor arrived little Stew was over the worst and breathing again quite normally. I must have passed out then, from sheer relief, I suppose, for I came round to find Jean holding my head down between my knees.

"He's all right, hen," she said, "but golly! it was a near thing!"

We never found out how the door of the greenhouse was left open, but all my former suspicion of Posy returned.

I could not prove it but I suspected that she had left the greenhouse door open, probably unintentionally. Thank heavens, I had noticed it and got there in time to save him. Mrs. Tucker did not agree with me, and her face was stony as she said in an icy voice, "I'm going to ring Miss Jenner at once." I wondered why.

When Miss Jenner arrived, I was sent to make some

tea, and as I approached the room with the tray in my hands I heard Mrs. Tucker say, "I don't say the fault was hers, Elspeth is too fond of Stewart to want to harm him, but . . . well, she is such a strange girl and seems to bring bad luck with her, misfortunes follow her in a frightening way . . . I've had as much as I can stand. I'm sorry, Miss Jenner, but there it is, she'll have to go."

I gasped and nearly dropped the tray—she was blaming me!

Miss Jenner sipped her tea thoughtfully, her face grave, and when Mrs. Tucker left us she turned a worried and puzzled look on me. "Oh Elphie," she sighed, "I can't understand it!"

"They don't want to adopt me, do they?" I prompted. "She blames *me* for what happened to little Stew."

"I'm afraid that's right, Elphie," Miss Jenner answered, "and they don't want to keep you here any longer. Mrs. Tucker has asked me to take you away at once. Are you certain that you didn't leave that greenhouse door open by mistake?"

"*I* certainly DID NOT!" I shouted at her. "It's wicked of her to suggest such a thing. I had nothing to do with it, he'd have been dead if I hadn't *found* him! Oh, how can I leave little Stew?" I wailed jumping to my feet. "I can't! I just *can't!*"

"I'm afraid you must, Elphie," said Miss Jenner quietly. "Mrs. Tucker won't let you have anything more to do with him. *I* believe you, but I think Mrs. Tucker is really frightened—I told you the village was an odd one, superstitious, unenlightened. I'll come and help you to pack your things, and we'll leave at once."

At her bleak words and the thought of leaving the

little boy I loved, something seemed to snap in my mind, all my vitality drained out of me, my legs gave way and I crumpled down onto the floor.

Miss Jenner's face wavered over me through a white fog, voices came and went and I was lifted onto the couch; a cup was held to my lips and I swallowed as I was told. Then I was budled into a car, still in a dreamlike state.

"I'm all right," I found myself repeating, "all right . . . all right."

"Of course you are, Elphie." Miss Jenner's reassuring voice came through to me. "I'm taking you home with me now, dear, so stop worrying."

When we reached her house I floated up the stairs to the little pink and white room I had occupied after Grannie Gil died. I was put to bed and Miss Jenner fussed over me—it was all part of a dream, quite unreal, but I wanted it to go on for I knew that when it came to an end I would have to face reality.

Miss Jenner kept me in bed and sent for the doctor, who prescribed rest and care and a selection of pills.

I slept and slept, and the longer I slept the more tired and lifeless I felt. Once again I was homeless, unwanted, rejected, with no place of my own. Why? What was there wrong with me? Most of all I grieved for the loss of little Stew, for now I had no one to love.

"Perhaps we should try to find your mother?" Miss Jenner suggested.

"No! Oh no! Never!" I cried violently. "I won't ever see her again whatever happens!" I was absolutely determined about this for she had been the first to reject me, and I blamed her for my father's mental collapse.

Miss Jenner really did her best for me. She provided me with books, with radio and music, she gave me the shelter of her home when I needed a refuge, she protected me from contact with the outside world at a time when I felt terrified of people and the hurt they could inflict on me. As long as I was in her home I felt safe. I knew that she could not keep me permanently, but I trusted her enough to believe that she'd find a solution for me.

Her friend, Dr. Winter, who came to see her one day, was a big clumsy-looking woman, but somehow persuasive for I found myself answering the questions she asked me, I felt she really cared what became of me.

It was at her suggestion that Miss Jenner made inquiries about a very special children's home, a place where they took in children who were emotionally disturbed, children who needed time and care to recover from some shattering experience or disaster.

"They say they can find a corner for you, Elphie, till you are able to go back to ordinary life again. What about it, will you give it a try? It really *is* a nice place."

I thought it over in silence. The idea of a special place, a refuge, appealed to me—there seemed to be no alternative anyway. I had no choice so I agreed to go. Somewhere had to be found for me, it might as well be a children's home and this sounded like a good one. But however pleasant it turned out to be, I was determined to keep to my tough image; no one would get to know the real me. I vowed to keep everyone at a distance and trust no one.

Part Two

Chapter Eleven

I was rather daunted at first sight by the grandeur of the old house with its little stone turrets and tiny slit windows high in the thick walls—Barnalogie—it was to be my home for many months.

Miss Jenner came with me to settle me in as she said and handed me over to Matron, a cosy, comfortable-looking person.

"I'll put you in with two other girls," Matron told me, "or if you'd rather have a room to yourself, there is one free."

"P- p- put me by myself," I said sharply, embarrassed at the recurrence of my stammer. Matron was unperturbed. "Right," she said. "Now, how about a cup of coffee?"

She poured one for each of us and sat down beside Miss Jenner, while I took mine to the window seat and looked across the yard to the opposite wing of the house with its grim little stone turrent and narrow window.

The sun was on it, spotlighting it, and just for a second the curtain twitched and a face peered out at me, then vanished.

A pity the room was already occupied, I thought. I'd have liked it for myself.

Presently Matron took us along to the Common Room to meet some of the other children. It was an attractive, bright room, with comfortable chairs, paintings on the walls and shelves of books. Several girls and boys in their early teens were seated about the room, and the loud rhythmic beat of pop throbbed from a record player in one corner.

"You should all be outside on this lovely day," Matron remarked. "Here is Elspeth Harrier, who is coming to join us for a while—Elphie."

She named each of the others, but none of them showed any interest in me beyond a slight nod. I scowled at them.

"Now we'll have a look at your bedroom, shall we?" said Matron. "This way."

She bustled up a staircase and along a passage and stopped outside the open door of a small bedroom. The walls were painted a soft Chinese blue, the bedcover and curtains were a lovely cherry color, and the window looked out onto the garden. I was enchanted by it, but I certainly wasn't going to show it.

"Yes, it's not bad," I said grudgingly. Matron appeared not to notice my churlishness.

"I'll send someone along with your case, and she'll help you to unpack and settle in," she said briskly, "then she can bring you along to my office to say goodbye to Miss Jenner."

As soon as they'd gone, I sat down on the bed and looked around me admiring the room. It was just right, and I was so pleased I felt like purring!

Chapter Eleven

In a few minutes there was a knock at the door and a girl staggered in with my two cases.

"Hello," she said, "I'm Mac."

"Hello," I grunted and took the cases from her. She looked terribly thin and not much older than myself, not old enough to be on the staff. Her jeans were very much patched and she was wearing an ugly purple shirt, which did nothing for her appearance, and her hair looked lank and uncared for, but not as ugly as mine.

"I'm leaving here very soon," she said confidingly. "They're waiting for me in Hollywood—I've got an important part in a film."

For a moment I was astonished but believed her. "What is your film name?" I asked.

"Brigitte Bardot," she said, so I knew her story was a pack of lies, her imagination out of control.

I nodded as if I believed her. "I'd better get on with my unpacking," I said, turning my back on her.

"Yes, I'll help you," she offered. "I shan't be here next week. I'm going to my grandmother's before I leave for America."

Barnalogie was well-organized and orderly, I liked that, it gave me a feeling of security. In the mornings there were classes as in an ordinary school, taken by two resident teachers. In the afternoon we chose what we wanted to do: woodwork, pottery, weaving, painting, music, gardening, dressmaking, cooking. Visiting teachers came to take those classes. There were pets to be cared for: rabbits, guinea pigs, kittens, several goats and a donkey. There were quite a number of helpers, some of whom came daily from the village, including

Mr. McCann the gardener and handyman, a curious troll-like character, gruff and unapproachable.

Barnalogie was a very free sort of place, within its sheltering walls no one bothered us. There were set times for meals and classes and bedtime, but apart from those we were free to do what we liked in the house and grounds.

There were about twenty-five of us girls and boys, mostly in our early teens though a few were older. Although we lived in a community there was little real communication between us, few friendships were formed; all of us were damaged children, each one isolated by her own troubles—detached, self-contained, solitary, deliberately unattractive, and this suited me very well just then. Perhaps like me they trusted no one—not even Matron—afraid of the hurt that other human beings can inflict, avoiding close contact in case it should end in pain and rejection. But we all suffered from an overwhelming loneliness; however kind and concerned the workers in Barnalogie were, none of us *belonged* to any of them, none of us belonged to *anyone*.

During one of Miss Jenner's visits she told me that my father might have to have a brain operation, which the doctors hoped would help him. "You could write to him again, poor man, couldn't you Elphie?" she suggested. But I didn't, I was too mean to bother. I felt he had been lost to me for too long, my feelings for him were frozen.

Parting with little Stew had caused me such pain that I still felt numb. I must not let myself be drawn close to anyone again. I had to get used to being without love, to being a loner.

Ever since I had arrived at Barnalogie, the room in the turret of the house had intrigued me. But when I asked who it belonged to, I was told that no one lived in that oldest part of the house, the room had been empty for years. Yet, I *knew* I had seen the curtain twitched and a face peering out at me, just for an instant, the day I arrived. Once when I was working in the garden with Mr. McCann I asked him about the turret room. He gave me a startled look and wagged a warning finger at me. "Ye'd better keep yer distance from that part of the house, lassie," he said in his surliest voice.

Naturally this intrigued me, for Mr. McCann belonged to the village and must have known the house all his life. But I asked him no more at the time and pretended to have lost interest, for he was an uncommunicative old man and did not encourage chatter. But I began to plan how to get into that turret room.

One day my chance came when there was a birthday party in the garden. I slipped away to the house while some games were going on so that no one would notice my absence. I stole round the house till I came to the turret, but its strong wooden door, studded with rusty nails, was locked. I hunted around for a few minutes, hoping to find a key hidden somewhere close to it; I felt along the edge of the stone above the door, which I could just reach by standing on tiptoe, but I had no luck.

It was such a narrow little turret that I was sure there

was a spiral staircase inside it, mounting to the room at the top. Surely there must be another way into it from inside the house. Obviously I was not going to get in from the outside without asking Matron or someone for the key, and I meant to keep my interest in the turret room secret. I decided to explore the inside of the house near the turret more thoroughly and try to find an entrance.

It was as I stood outside the door gazing up at the window of the turret room that for the second time I saw the curtain twitch, and for an instant a face looked down at me—more the *shape* of a face really, for it was very hazy, but I thought it looked old and hostile. As I blinked it was gone, and the curtain was back in place again.

Chapter Twelve

Now that I knew there was someone using the turret room, I was more determined than ever to find my way into it. But first I had to discover who the occupant was; one of the cleaning women who came from the village perhaps, or someone who came to sew or mend?

I made several careful inquiries among the cleaners but always got the same reply. "No one's been in that old turret for years!"

It was very mysterious, but curiosity spurred me on. I had to discover the way in and find out who the inhabitant was, for I wanted the room for myself.

My first move was to spend more time in my bedroom, reading or working, so that my disappearances from the Common Room would not be thought strange and it would be assumed that I was in an extra anti-social mood and would be left alone.

Then I had to borrow a torch from Matron, for how could I find my way up into the turret without a light? From my bedroom it was easy to slip along the corridor to the old part of the house when no one was about, and to hunt around for a door leading into the turret. I searched every time I had a chance. I came to know the old part of the house well. But there was no sign of a door.

I must have passed the broom cupboard a dozen times before I thought of examining its walls thoroughly, and it was there I finally found a little door hidden under the brushes and cleaning things. It had a bolt, but no keyhole or doorknob. The bolt was rusty and it took a lot of patience to get it loose. The door, when at last I got it open, creaked abominably—Mr. McCann's oil can would put that right—but it *was* the door I had hoped for, the one that led into the turret! I had no time to explore further that day. I had to content myself with a quick flash of the torch, which showed a little stone staircase spiraling upward through the turret, up to the intriguing room at the top.

I drew a deep breath of excitement and pleasure and closed the door softly behind me, coaxing the bolt back into place and leaving the broom cupboard as I'd found it. Then I hurried downstairs to join the others for supper.

I had to wait a couple of days before I could explore further, then a wet afternoon gave me the chance I needed.

"I'm going to read in my room for a while," I announced brusquely in the Common Room. "It's too noisy here."

"Very well," said Matron, who happened to be there, "but come down in about an hour. I'm organizing a competition."

I ran upstairs to my bedroom and left a book open

on the bed. Then I tiptoed along the deserted corridor to the broom cupboard, where I shut the door behind me. I had brought the torch with me and Mr. McCann's smallest oil can, and I soon found the little door in the back wall, gently pushed it open and oiled its hinges.

There was a smell of dust and damp, fustiness, . . . and something else—hostility.

The little stone staircase spiraled upwards, lit by a slit of window in the wall of the turret. Carefully I mounted the worn steps till I reached the threshold of the room at the top. It had no door, but something held me on the top step preventing me from entering the room as surely as if the occupant stood before me barring the way in. But there was no occupant, the room was completely empty. The fustiness was very strong, almost repellent, and such vibrations of hostility emanated from the walls that for a moment I was daunted and almost turned back. Then my courage returned and I tried a firm approach.

"I'm coming in," I said aloud in a purposeful voice. There was a slight shift in the air of the room, an added coldness, the hostility was still strong, but the threshold was no longer barred.

"That's better," I said, took a step forward and stood inside the turret room.

The walls were bare and rounded like a windmill or a lighthouse, the furnishings were sparse—a bed, a table, a chest, a stool and a rocking chair. Cobwebs draped the walls and the room was very dusty, a dreary room and quite uninviting. The air was stale though cold, as if no window had been opened for a very long time. A grubby curtain of lace hung over the glass and

I longed to twitch it and peep out, but I was afraid of being seen from the outside.

Yet, however unprepossessing it looked, the room appealed to me; in it I could be quite alone and undisturbed, secret and solitary. I would clean it, freshen it and make it my own. Unless someone did an unusual amount of checking up on me, which was most unlikely, I could count on being undiscovered, hidden; no one would know where I was. But before I could make the room my own and feel able to relax in it, I had to come to terms with its occupant. I had to find a way of overcoming the hostility, the uneasy atmosphere, for I felt myself bitterly resented. I must try to get to know whoever used the room. There must be someone; I had not imagined that face at the window—but who could it be? And how was I to find out? I sat down on the stool to think, and I remembered what Mr. McCann had said about the old wing of the house. "Ye'd better keep yer distance from it, lassie."

So there must be some story or gossip circulating in the village, something that Mr. McCann knew about. I must get to know him better and persuade him to tell me about Barnalogie.

It was very still, very eerie as I sat listening to the steady drip of the rain. I felt increasingly uneasy as if someone were watching me with malevolent eyes, almost holding me under a spell that kept me rooted to the stool.

At last with a great effort I made myself rise and stumble across the room, my feet felt heavy as stone, but I knew I must get out as quickly as possible, the atmosphere was alive with threat, although there was no one there.

But when I reached the doorway and turned to take a last look at the room . . . I saw that the rocking chair was moving rhythmically, steadily, as if someone or something had just that moment risen from it. . . .

Chapter Thirteen

For a day or two I did not venture near the turret room. I had been quite badly frightened and needed time to recapture my courage. But the room held a strange fascination for me, curiosity nagged at me compelling me to go back to investigate its mystery, and eventually my inquisitiveness overcame my fear.

I chose a sunny evening around six, before the light began to dim, and I climbed the spiral stair with caution, prepared for anything to happen. The room was bathed in golden light and as I stepped into it there was no prohibition, no antagonism as before . . . the room was utterly empty and at peace. An idea came to me, and I returned quickly to the broom cupboard and brought back with me a dustpan and brush and a duster. I dealt with the cobwebs and the worst of the dust, and when I had finished, the room looked a lot better. I even risked trying to open the window, but the hinge was rusty and I made a mental note to bring the oil can again on my next visit. Every now and then from the corner of my eye I looked toward the rocking chair half expecting to catch a movement, but there was none.

Chapter Thirteen

By the time I was ready to go, the sun was very low and shadows were beginning to darken the room, but there was still nothing to disquiet or alarm me. I crept down the stair and returned the cleaning things to the cupboard, then feeling slightly disappointed at the negativeness of my reception, I made my way down to the Common Room to join the others for supper.

My third visit was at dusk and I went armed with an oil can, a bucket of soapy water, a scrubbing brush, a tin of polish and a bundle of cloths—the broom cupboard had its uses. Then I really got down to work. I even washed the windowpanes and the grubby curtain. When I had finished, the little room really shone, and I felt pleased with it and hoped soon to be able to use it myself, when I had met and dealt with its inhabitant. Like the last time, there had been no watcher, the room had been empty.

Then the very last moment, as I gathered up my cleaning things and was about to leave, there was a sudden coldness in the room and a wave of animosity hit me like a hammer, so strong it was. Startled I backed out onto the stair, clutching my bucket and brushes, and almost fell backwards down the stone steps. The room repulsed me as an unwelcome intruder, hostility was strongly there once more.

But I refused to be put off by the mysterious inmate. The subtle spell of uncertainty intrigued me, especially as I had begun to believe that whoever occupied the room was not human. Also, I coveted that room. I needed it for my own use, and I was determined to have it.

A few days later when I was walking through a

marshy part of the little wood beyond the paddock I
came upon a colony of those lovely white flowers—Grass
of Parnassus. It had been one of my father's favorites,
and we had often found it growing by the little pool
where he used to fish, beyond High Stair. There were
plenty of them so I picked a little bunch and took them
back to my bedroom to stand in a jam jar on my table.
I looked with delight at the delicate green veining on
the white petals, at the green heart of the flower surrounded by golden stamens—they reminded me of
happy times with my father. But the memories made
me sad, too, and suddenly I felt a need to be really
alone; I hurried to the stairs in the cupboard and
went up.

The turret room when I stepped into it was palely
sunlit, but its smiling appearance was false, there was
no welcome. I felt almost forcibly unwanted, resented.
But it all smelled fresh and clean, the old furniture
shone with my polishing, and although the room looked
bare, it was no longer dingy and dirty.

I sat down on the stool to admire my handiwork, and
almost at once the rocking chair began to creak slightly.
As I watched it, a shadowy figure began to take shape—
the figure of an old woman in old-fashioned clothes,
sitting in the chair, gently rocking. After a few minutes
I saw her more clearly, her long thin face, her gray hair
piled high on her head, while her slim foot in its black-
buttoned shoe soundlessly tapped the floor. But it was
to her hands that my attention was particularly drawn,
for she kept twisting them on her lap as if in great
agitation, as Grannie Gil used to do when she was badly
upset.

Chapter Thirteen

It was then that I lost my fear and began to feel sorry for her, she looked harmless enough, though unfriendly and rather haughty. I wondered what had distressed her so much? Suddenly I understood—my presence in the room was upsetting her. It was *her* room, and I had invaded her privacy uninvited. I must think of something to placate her, something to show her that I meant her no harm. I looked around the room for inspiration and quickly it came to me. I ran down to my bedroom and returned with my jar of wild flowers and set them on the table. "These are for you," I said softly, and I sat down on the stool by her side.

Immediately I felt a change in the atmosphere of the room, a lessening of tension, a relaxing of hostility, and the shadowy figure in the chair became clearer, less nebulous, so that I could see her in more detail. Her stern face was very pale, like a plant that has been kept too long in the dark, but as the mournful eyes looked straight at me, her expression softened, she half-smiled at me, and a tear slid down her cheek. I was torn with pity for her; she was old, frailer than Grannie Gil, and she looked so sad and forlorn.

"I didn't know this room is yours," I said. "I'm sorry I distressed you by breaking into it. I won't come again if you don't want me to, but if you're as lonely as I am, perhaps you'll allow me to share it with you?" She sat without moving for a moment, then slightly inclined her head—it could hardly be called a nod. Then leaving the chair gently rocking, she vanished. It was the beginning of our strange friendship. I was fascinated by her and also slightly scared. I had never met a ghost before and I didn't know what might happen.

After she had left me I began to think how extraordinary the whole thing was. Here was I actually talking to a ghost, involving myself with her, wanting to cheer her up, to give her pleasure.

Who was she, I wondered, and what kept her in that comfortless room?

Somehow I would have to persuade Mr. McCann to tell me about her, for I was sure that he knew her story, but it was going to be difficult to get him to talk, taciturn as he was. Perhaps if I were to talk more to *him*, thaw him out as it were by taking more interest in gardening, get him to explain to me his skills in the greenhouse, I could lead him on with subtle questioning till I had found out what I wanted.

Chapter Fourteen

I started on Mr. McCann the very next day; whenever I had any time to spare I dashed out into the garden or the greenhouses and got him to explain to me what he was doing and why. I came to enjoy working with him and I got really interested and learned a lot from him about growing things.

His knowledge was wider than Grannie Gil's, and he used different methods from hers, but sometimes he allowed me to try her treatment of a certain flower and was pleased when I had a success. I began to tell him about Grannie Gil and her garden; because he was an unsociable person like myself, I did not mind talking to Mr. McCann. Gradually he got used to my chatter and even seemed to enjoy my tales about Grannie. "She must have been a gey fine lady," he remarked once, "ye'll miss her sorely, lassie."

"Yes I do," I replied.

Soon I began to ask him about the village when he was young, and about its people; sometimes he answered my questions and sometimes he didn't, but I had succeeded in getting him to talk at last.

Later on Matron remarked on how much healthier I looked and encouraged me to be out of doors as much as possible. This left me less time to spend on visits to the turret room, but I still went up there as often as I could. Nothing barred my way now, the antagonism had gone, I had been accepted. Sometimes the old woman was there in her rocking chair, sometimes not, but even when the room was empty I tried to bring something with me each time I visited it, something colorful or beautiful to brighten it for us both. Sometimes it was flowers I brought, sometimes a picture I had painted or cut out to stick on the wall. Once I brought a gaily striped cover I had made for the table, once a little silk cushion for the rocking chair that I had bought at one of the jumble sales which were held from time to time in our stables. I managed to make the room quite home-like and that pleased the old lady.

Then one day when he was in a good mood, I began to talk to Mr. McCann about Barnalogie.

"It's a fine house, who did it belong to?" I asked.

"To a family called Seaton," he said. "Aye it's a fine house, and in the old laird's time when my grandfather was head gardener it was a bonny place I can tell ye, plenty of young life about it, and no shortage of money."

"So what's happened to it?" I asked.

"The old laird died and his son was killed in the war —only the daughter was left, alone in the house, Miss Adela Seaton—Miss Ada—she lived in the turret room, shut away from everyone, poor soul."

"Why?" I asked, "why did she live in the turret room when the whole house belonged to her?"

Chapter Fourteen

"Well, she was short of money and the house fell into disrepair," said Mr. McCann, "and maybe she felt *safe* in the turret, ye see."

"I don't see—safe from what?" I asked.

Mr. McCann drove his fork deep into the earth once or twice before he answered, then glancing from side to side to make sure he was not overheard he whispered, "She had the evil eye."

"What d-do you m-m-mean?" I faltered.

"She ill-wished people, brought bad luck on them, her family, the servants, the village. Her father shut her away to keep her safe and to prevent her from doing harm. I suppose she got used to living in the turret room and chose to remain there. Nobody's been in it these many years—it's haunted, ye see, and better kept locked up, especially now that it's a children's home."

"You mean there's a ghost in the turret room?" I said softly.

Mr. McCann nodded. "Miss Ada's ghost," he whispered, "there's no dislodging her from that room, so the old folks in the village say."

"Do *you* believe that story, Mr. McCann?" I asked sceptically. "Do *you* believe she had the evil eye?"

"Maybe I do," he acknowledged, "and maybe I don't." Then changing his tone to one of impatience he turned on me. "I'd better get on with my work, and mind there's no tittle-tattling from you about what I've told ye!" he said.

He trudged away from me towards the tool shed, and I left my weeding and returned to the house.

I had learned what I wanted to know, my old woman was the sad ghost of Miss Ada Seaton, and no wonder

79

she was sad. I did not believe that she had the evil eye, she was probably as innocent as I was myself, we were both unlucky, that was all. But this made a bond between us. I felt an even greater sympathy for her and determined to try to please her, to make closer friends with her, for I knew she was as lonely as I was.

It was easier in the dusky evenings of the winter, when I had to be indoors anyway, to creep up unseen to the turret room. Sometimes it was quite dark, but I did not dare to take a light for fear of it showing outside. It was eerie at times, sitting in the dusk with a ghost, but I found it stimulating and exciting. Now that I knew her story and her name I felt a great interest in her. Miss Ada Seaton, Miss Ada—in my secret mind I always called her "Miss Ghost."

Later in the winter it was so bitterly cold in the turret room that I used to pull on a thick sweater when I went up there and I could not stay for long. Even when it was too dark to see her, I knew by the creaking of the rocking chair that she was there. I sat on the stool and talked to her. I told her about the happenings of the day, my triumphs and my failures, and sometimes I confided in her my secret thoughts and hopes . . .

"I wish I was ordinary," I said, "with a family and a home of my own where I belonged—that's my strongest wish, the one that matters most."

I continued to bring little gifts to brighten the room, and Miss Ada showed her pleasure by silently clapping her hands. As I talked, if I could see her face, I watched her expression for delight or disapproval, and a strange kind of communication developed between us, though she never spoke a word.

Chapter Fourteen

Once while she was rocking gently beside me I put out my hand in an affectionate gesture to pat her knee, and felt quite astonished when my hand passed right through her and touched the chair—she was so real to me that I sometimes forgot she was only a ghost.

I can't remember just when it was that I became interested in poetry and began writing my own poems. For some time I kept them secret, but soon I became so excited about them I had to tell someone, so I took them to the turret room and read them to Miss Ghost. I thought she liked them and I was encouraged to write more, and to tell her more and more about myself, confiding to her my private dreams. With her I felt completely safe, my trust in her could not be broken since she was no longer alive. Except for her I kept myself aloof, withdrawn, so that nobody knew the real me, not even Mr. McCann. I felt I had to protect myself from everyone else—even Matron—no one would have the power to hurt me again if I kept myself apart, isolated. This is what I really believed at the time.

Perhaps it was just as well I did not realize how much Matron knew about *me*, nor how often I gave myself away to her. Her carefully hidden concern for me was never evident, it was not until I had left Barnalogie that I discovered she knew most of what I had thought was secret; but she had respected my wish for solitude because she understood my need for it. I was not yet ready to return to normal relationships.

Restrictions and rules at Barnalogie were as few as possible; we had a feeling of freedom, we were unfettered. Mostly we lived within the extensive grounds, which covered acres of garden, paddock, woods and farmland, but we were encouraged to go to the shop in the village, with permission from Matron.

For some time I was content to stay in the garden and grounds, and much of my spare time was spent in the turret room, for my absorption with Miss Ada increased as I became more devoted to her and I grew more dependent on her companionship. In spite of Mr. McCann's stories, I doubt if she had ever harmed anyone, poor soul.

So throughout the winter I stayed within the shelter of Barnalogie and did not venture outside its gates. I had no wish to meet the world outside. I was still afraid of contact with strangers—in Barnalogie I felt safe and content. But I kept up my defenses. I did not suspect that they had already started to crumble. I hid behind a disagreeable appearance—a scowling face and an ugly cropped head.

Chapter Fifteen

There was only one thing about my visits to the turret room that worried me, and at first I did not pay it much attention. But soon it became so noticeable that I could not ignore it—an overwhelming tiredness descended on me after I had been in the room for a few minutes. I would arrive full of life and energy, but in no time I began to feel weary, lethargic, as if my vitality were oozing out of me. I had to get out of the room quickly before all my strength left me.

It didn't happen each time I went to the room, only sometimes, and before long I realized that it was only in the presence of Miss Ada that I became exhausted, when she was not there I was all right.

I thought about it a lot, and I began to wonder if she drew vitality from me, sapped my strength, drained me of energy. Did my presence give her some kind of life? She had certainly become more substantial than when I first saw her, her shape better defined, details like the buttons on her dress could be clearly seen, where before she had been almost transparent.

As the months went by, there were changes at Barnalogie; children left and others took their places. Gradually I became more friendly towards them all, though I did not allow any of them to come close to me; Miss Ghost was my friend and I needed no other. My secret relationship with her gave me confidence, however, and slowly I became easier and more relaxed, less difficult with Matron and the rest of the staff, more inclined to fit in with other people.

Although I did not confide in Matron, I listened to what she had to say to me. I had developed a great respect for her, I could almost say fondness, though I kept it secret.

So when she suggested that I should spread my wings a little, join one of the excursions by mini-bus to Edinburgh Castle, or to a Museum or Art Gallery with some of the other children, I did not refuse to listen as once I'd have done.

"Not that yet," I said. "Perhaps later on, but I might go to the village to buy one or two things, if you like."

"Yes, that's a good idea," said Matron approvingly, "what about going tomorrow morning, it's Saturday so you'll have no classes. Would you like to go with someone or on your own?"

I thought for a minute—it was a big step for me to leave the shelter of Barnalogie, could I face it alone?

"I think I'd like to try on my own," I said slowly.

"Good girl, Elphie," said Matron pleased. "I think you'll quite enjoy it. Make yourself look nice, won't you?"

I knew what she meant, so when I went to see her

next morning to tell her I was off, I wore a red woolly cap pulled well down over my hair.

"Pop into the post office for me and get a book of stamps, will you?" said Matron, and she handed me the money. "Don't be too long," she added. "You look fine."

It was a lovely morning, the April wind carried the bewitching scents of spring to me as I walked briskly down the drive and out of the gate of Barnalogie. Mr. McCann, who was pruning a hedge, greeted me with a wave of his hand as I passed him.

As soon as I was out of the gate, I saw the first cottages of the village ahead of me down the road; it was no distance to go. Blue wood smoke rose from the chimneys, and there was no one about, but as I drew nearer to the village my pace slowed and my heart began to beat faster. Then one or two people came out of the village store and I had to fight down my panic or I'd have turned and fled back to Barnalogie. I took a deep breath, walked steadily on and in a minute I was right in the village. I sauntered straight through it— there were only about eight or ten cottages and one or two bigger houses in pretty gardens at the far end. A little boy on a tricycle came flying out of a garden gate onto the path beside me, ringing his bell like mad. I jumped aside as he stopped dead with a screech of brakes.

"I nearly runned you over!" he exclaimed, his face red with excitement.

"Yes, but you didn't *quite* so it's OK," I answered. "Is it a new tricycle? It's a beauty."

"Yes, I just got it," he cried as he turned back into the garden and tore off towards the house.

I wandered back towards the shop again, the encounter with the little boy had somehow eased me so that I felt less pent up, less taut, and I managed to walk into the village store and respond to the "Good mornings" quite easily.

I bought a new pencil and a couple of exercise books for my poetry and a bar of chocolate, then I got Matron's stamps and left the shop quite pleased with myself.

Outside the sky had darkened and a shower threatened as I turned towards Barnalogie. As I approached the last cottage, where a woman stood leaning over the gate, and was about to hurry past her, the first heavy drops of rain began to fall and in a second there was a downpour.

"Better come in and shelter," she said to me, "quickly, or you'll be soaked!"

I hesitated for a moment, resisting the impulse to run for Barnalogie, then I dashed after her into the cottage.

We shook the rain off ourselves and she made me sit down by the fire to dry off.

I looked around the kitchen with its scrubbed wooden table, its pretty blue and white china on the dresser shelves, its windowsill clustered with pots of gay geraniums, its cat asleep on the basket armchair, its kettle simmering on the old-fashioned black stove—cosy, snug, comforting. I hadn't been inside anyone's home since I came to Barnalogie and it gave me a pang of homesickness, an ache for what I had lost. And when

Chapter Fifteen

I looked into the kindly face of the woman beside me
I saw nothing there to distrust, nothing but warmth
and friendliness.

"Ye'll take a cup of tea and one of my scones?" she
said.

"Oh . . . well . . . yes, thank you, I will," I said,
relaxing.

"I'm Mrs. McCann, and you'll be from Barnalogie
maybe?"

"Yes . . . I'm Elspeth Harrier. I know your husband. I often work in the garden with him," I said
eagerly.

"Aye, m'hm, I mind him speaking of you," said Mrs.
McCann.

She chattered away comfortably and presently the
sun came out again and I got up to go.

"Thank you very much," I said, "you're very kind,
Mrs. McCann."

"Come again, chuckie, when you're passing," she invited me.

I walked back to Barnalogie on light feet. Mr. Mc-
Cann was not in sight when I reached the gate so I
went straight to Matron to report my return and to
hand over her stamps.

"Well, and how did you get on, Elphie?" she asked
in her comfortable voice.

"Quite well, I enjoyed it," I told her, and described
my meeting with the little boy and with Mrs. McCann.

"That's very good," said Matron approvingly. "Well
done. You'll soon find it quite easy to go further afield.
You're getting better, Elphie, really better. We'll be
losing you soon now that you're looking so well—hap-

pier too, and I'm glad. You're becoming a pretty girl too, your coloring is lovely and so would your hair be, if you'd give it a chance! Now what about trying to make a friend here, even one friend; will you do that?"

She had said the wrong thing and my face closed against her. I did not want another friend. I had Miss Ghost; she was the only friend I needed, the tie between her and me was the only one I trusted—but of course Matron knew nothing of this. But I realized that she really cared about me and wanted to help me, and I was flattered by what she had said about my looks. Perhaps to please her I would let my hair grow and sometimes wear something nicer than jeans.

Later in the day I crept up to the turret room to tell Miss Ghost about my expedition. I sat in the dusty sunbeams while beyond me in the shadow she rocked to and fro. Something must have displeased her for she showed her agitation by frenzied rocking, and as my story continued her face became more and more disapproving. Something I had said must have offended her, but what?

Gradually lethargy overtook me as I sat there. I became drowsy and weak and felt myself relaxing into a kind of nothingness, my energy, my willpower draining out of me . . .

I was saved by the loud ringing of the supper bell that shocked me out of the dreamlike stupor into which I had fallen. I dragged myself upright and stumbled from the room, aware of some danger only half-understood, some threat that I could not name.

Chapter Sixteen

It was a day or two before I returned to the turret room. Something new and disturbing in Miss Ada's attitude to me had developed and I wanted to puzzle out what it meant before I saw her again. What had caused her displeasure?

After a lot of thinking I decided that she was jealous. She had not been pleased to hear of my visit to Mrs. McCann and my meeting with the little boy in the village, she wanted to keep me entirely to herself—her friend; she was becoming too possessive of me and this frightened me, for if she became too demanding I knew that I would have to break with her, and what would happen then?

When next I went up into the turret room it was shortly after lunch and I carried my mug of coffee up with me. I sat down in my usual place and began to drink it, but the room remained empty; Miss Ada was not there, the rocking chair was still, the air dormant, undisturbed.

I finished my coffee to the last sip then carelessly

glanced into the mug—the face mirrored at the bottom of it was not my own face . . . it was Miss Ada's.

Shocked I looked behind me expecting to see her peering over my shoulder into the mug, she was not there, yet the face staring back at me was *hers*, not mine!

I shut my eyes in a sudden panic, and when I looked again the face reflected back at me . . . was my own.

I took a deep breath to steady myself and fled down the stairs, through the house, and burst into the Common Room with its chatter and noise—for once I was glad of human company.

The incident bothered me a lot, what could it mean? Had I become so obsessed by Miss Ada that I was even beginning to *look* like her? Or was it a warning that if I persisted in deliberately isolating myself from other people I would become like her, a sad, lost person? Whatever the explanation the experience scared me—something must be done to break her spell over me. I had become too much involved with her, it was time I detached myself, developed some independence. I did not mean to waste my life as Miss Ada had hers, I wanted to *make* something of myself. But I was not ready to break with her entirely, I still needed her friendship. Perhaps I should take Matron's advice and make a friend of one of the other children at Barnalogie.

Although none of them appealed much to me, I did not really *know* any of them; although we shared a common roof, we mostly remained detached. We were a group of loners at Barnalogie, thrown together by our misfortunes, sharing the contacts of daily life, but our histories were unknown to one another, we did not discuss our problems.

The only one who interested me as I looked around for a possible friend, was a boy, Joseph Poynter, Jo-Jo, who had a communication problem and would not speak. He was younger than me, just about my brother Edward's age, and once I really looked at him his waif-like face and velvet dark eyes melted my heart towards him.

I had noticed that Jo-Jo had begun to hang about the greenhouse when I was in there potting out seedlings for Mr. McCann. He kept his distance, but he seemed interested. I had been ignoring him, but after that frightening day in the tower I asked him in to help me. He was very willing and soon I found myself teaching him the jobs that Mr. McCann left me to do. That was the start of it, and soon he was working eagerly along with Mr. McCann and myself, developing the same love for growing things as we had—but he never spoke a word.

One day I discovered by chance that Jo-Jo suffered from epileptic fits and this shook me, for I had begun to feel some responsibility for him and wondered if he should be working as hard as he did. I went to Matron and she told me how to cope with him if he had a sudden fit. "Be good to him, Elphie," she said, "he has had a bad time, poor little chap."

"Can you tell me anything about him?" I asked, for I knew one was never supposed to ask questions about another child.

"You must keep this to yourself, Elphie. His father is in prison—a long sentence, and his mother died only a few months ago. He has no one now, and you could help him, which is why I'm telling you about him. You'll have to be patient with him, he's difficult and moody, but I'm very glad you're taking an interest in him, he needs a friend. Keep it up, Elphie, and try to get him to talk to you."

"I'll try," I said, and I meant it, for I felt great sympathy for him, he was alone in the world like me.

It took me a long time to break his silence and get him to speak to me, but I was rewarded when he managed his first few words, and soon he was able to talk again, though his sentences were short and disjointed.

As my contact with Jo-Jo developed, I found myself wanting to meet other people, to get out of Barnalogie as Matron had suggested. I asked to join some of the expeditions she arranged and I decided to go into the village oftener. I found it quite easy once I started, and Matron was pleased with me. Soon I was visiting Mrs. McCann two or three times a week, and she regaled me with all the local gossip, it was a much nicer village than the Tuckers' one.

But when I tried to bring the conversation round to Miss Ada Seaton, Mrs. McCann seemed unwilling to talk about her.

"Let's talk about something pleasanter than that nasty old woman," she said.

Nasty? I thought, It's not what I would call her! Perhaps she only shows her nicest side to me. How wrong gossip can be.

Chapter Sixteen

Soon I got to know a number of the village people and stopped to chat with them—the postman Mr. McAlister, Old Grunty who collected the pig food and had only one tooth in his head; Miss Gerda, who'd come from Austria before the last war and still spoke with a foreign accent, but dressed dolls most beautifully; and lastly Sergeant McBane, the policeman. I knew them all as nice, friendly people whom I had come to like and trust.

"Mr. Colquhoun the artist lives in the big house at the far end of the village," Mr. McCann had informed me. "He paints grand pictures; I wish I could buy one."

I walked past the house several times to have a good look—I had never met an artist—and then one day as I approached its gate once more, a tiny kitten shot out of the garden and dashed across the road. It was too small to be out alone and I was hesitating, wondering whether to go after it, when a furious barking broke out. I ran towards the noise and saw the kitten perched on the top of a garden wall, shivering with fright while an Alsatian with snapping jaws jumped higher and higher trying to reach it. I just managed to stretch up far enough to reach the trembling little creature, snatched it down and tucked it inside my waistcoat; luckily the dog could not get out of the garden. Then I walked up the drive of the artist's house and boldly rang the bell. The door was opened by a boy a little older than myself, fourteen perhaps.

He saw the kitten and held out his hands to take it.

"Oh, Catapult! You naughty kitten! Did he run off again? He's always doing it."

"Yes, and that Alsatian might have got him; he's a vicious dog," I cried, pointing along the road to the wall.

"Thank you very much for rescuing Catapult and bringing him home," said the boy.

"What's going on?" a voice demanded and a pretty dark-haired woman appeared.

"Mum, that wicked kitten got out again and this kind girl saved him from being eaten by the Caldwell's Alsatian and brought him home."

"Oh, thank you—thank you very much. This is my son Patrick—Pad. Our name is Colquhoun. Do come in won't you?"

"I'm . . . El . . . Elspeth H-Harrier," I began, but I was so upset at my wretched stammer starting again that I just gulped and couldn't go on.

"Pad, take Elspeth into the kitchen and give her some coffee," said Mrs. Colquhoun. "I'll join you in a few minutes."

"Come on," said the boy, and he led the way into a big, airy room, bright with color and with wide windows looking out onto an orchard.

"What a marvelous room for a k-kitchen," I cried.

"It's more than kitchen; everything goes on in here," said the boy. "Look, sit down and I'll get you a cup of coffee. Here, Catapult, you can go to sleep for a bit." He put the kitten gently into his basket, and I sat down on a bench at a long wooden table by the window.

He poured two cups of coffee from a jug on the stove and sat down opposite me. "Biscuits in the box," he said pushing it towards me, "help yourself."

Along one wall was a splendid painting of a harbor

dotted with boats with brilliantly colored sails and the
sea shimmering into the distant sky.

"I like that," I remarked. "Who painted it?"

"My father, Driscoll Colquhoun," said the boy
proudly.

"Of course—the artist—I've heard of him in the village."

"You don't live here, do you? Are you visiting
friends?" he asked.

"I . . . I . . . I'm staying at Barnalogie," I said,
suddenly shy.

He looked up and straight at me. "It must be quite
. . . interesting to stay there for a little while," he
commented. "Have you been ill? You don't look it."

"Well . . . sort of," I replied, "but I'm better now."

"So you'll be going home soon?" he suggested en-
couragingly.

"I . . . I don't know," I said lamely, not knowing
how to answer him.

"Elspeth's at Barnalogie, Mum," said the boy as his
mother came in, "but she's OK again now."

"That's good," said Mrs. Colquhoun briskly. "It's a
wonderful place, most unusual. I suppose you'll be going home again soon, but come in and see us anytime
you like, and perhaps my husband will be here."

"Thank you, I'd like to," I said as I got up to go. "I
hope Catapult will be all right."

"I'm sure he will, thanks to you," said Mrs. Colquhoun. "Pad, take Elspeth to the gate."

We walked down the drive together and he opened
the gate for me.

"D'you paint, like your father?" I asked.

"A little, do you?" I shook my head and blurted out, "I write poetry—a little."

"Well, I hope we'll see you again before you go home —where is your home?" Pad asked.

There was a silence and I saw Pad looking at me in a concentrated way, as if trying to see me not only with his eyes but with his understanding.

"I haven't got a home," I murmured at last, "not anymore."

"Oh . . . Elspeth . . . I'm truly sorry, I didn't know . . . " He sounded distressed.

"It's all right," I said. "I'll go now," and I walked quickly away.

Chapter Seventeen

Inexplicably, I did not resent having given myself away to Pad, although we were new to one another. I felt that I could trust him, he seemed really concerned about me, he was gentle and kind and gave the impression of caring.

After tea I went up to the turret room to tell Miss Ada about my outing—some of it. I decided not to tell her about the time I had spent in the Colquhoun's house, for it seemed to me to be everything that a home should be, everything that I'd want *my* home to be, and I did not want Miss Ada's jealousy to spoil the picture. Her face was eager, greedy almost, and she seemed to hang on my words as I told her about the kitten and the Alsatian. She nodded her approval as I described the scene and was avid for more of the story, but I did not want to mention Pad or his mother to her, for I remembered how jealously she had reacted to Mrs. McCann. I ended my story abruptly, "I rang the doorbell and handed the kitten in . . . and here I am back again."

Even as I finished speaking, the usual lethargy began to creep over me and I think I must have fallen asleep for a few minutes for I had a monstrous dream. In it Miss Ada and I had changed places, she was young and powerful while *I*, dwindled and shrunken, was the poor ghost in the rocking chair.

The sun was gone when I woke and the room was cold but empty. All my confidence had vanished, ebbed away from me—how had I ever imagined that the Colquhouns really wanted me to come again, would be glad to see me. They were only being polite and did not really mean their invitation to be accepted. I had better stick to Miss Ada, I knew I could count on her even if I felt a bit smothered by her at times; she was my best, my only friend.

But I was wrong. A letter came for me next day from Mrs. Colquhoun asking me to tea the following Saturday. My heart lifted with pleasure and I took the letter to show to Matron.

"There, Elphie," she exclaimed beaming, "didn't I tell you you'd soon make friends outside—and the Colquhouns are fine people. You'll go, won't you? It will be lovely for you."

But I hesitated and hung back—landing casually on them was one thing, but a written invitation when I was expected and prepared for was quite another and I wondered if I could manage it. Perhaps I'd better stay inside Barnalogie's sheltering walls after all.

"I'll have to think about it," I said, "it would be nice to go . . . but. . . ."

"But nothing!" Matron broke in. "They like you and want to see you, Elphie—just you sit down here and write straightaway that you'll come."

Chapter Seventeen

So, I did, and through the days that followed, the thought of seeing Pad again, of being with that charming family cheered me like a candle flame in a darkened window.

I did not neglect Miss Ada, but neither did I tell her about my Saturday invitation.

When the day arrived I was keyed up and almost sick with excitement and apprehension—supposing it all went wrong and I was a flop?

I took a long time to dress, choosing my prettiest frock and wishing I had something new to wear. Then I washed and brushed my hair, which now curled round my face, till it shone like silk; and as excitement had brought color to my cheeks I really looked not so bad.

"You look great, Elphie!" Matron exclaimed when I popped into her office to say goodbye.

"I'd like to learn to do dressmaking," I said abruptly. "I've got nothing decent to wear."

If Matron was astonished she didn't show it. "You're quite right," she agreed. "You need some new clothes, pretty ones. You can start classes in dressmaking as soon as you like. Now off you go and have a good time."

I set off down the drive, but as I drew nearer to the gate my steps slowed. I felt reluctant to leave the security of Barnalogie, perhaps I'd be a disappointment after all, perhaps I'd better turn back.

But I could see in the distance the Colquhouns' house waiting for me, promising me something precious, something wonderful, and my courage rose as I stepped out through the gates—and there was Pad, come to meet me.

"Oh!" I gasped. "I wasn't expecting you . . . I . . ."

"I was afraid you might change your mind about coming," he said teasingly.

"Would that have mattered much?" I murmured.

"Of course it would . . . shocking bad manners," he said laughing.

But I sensed that he was serious, he really *did* want to see me so he must like me a little at least.

"How's Catapult?" I asked as we swung along the village street together.

"Naughty as ever," Pad answered. "My father, Drisc, is at home today so you'll meet him. I'm an only, you see, that's why they sent me to boarding school."

"What's it like at boarding school?" I asked.

"Not bad—what's it like at Barnalogie?"

"Not bad," I answered, and we both laughed.

"*Why* are you there—you're not ill . . . or dotty?" he said, suddenly serious.

"I was a bit . . . peculiar for a time. I had to go *somewhere* after my grandmother died," I explained, "and the foster parents I went to didn't want to adopt me."

"Oh, I see," said Pad gravely, but I didn't believe he *could* see, mine was such a different world from his.

"It's too early to go in," Pad remarked when we reached his home. "Let's walk a bit—there's something I want to show you."

"OK," I said. "Let's leave the main road—not that it's very busy."

"Yes, we'll go straight on toward the woods and the river," Pad explained; "the main road from the village goes off to the right."

Chapter Seventeen

When we went down the hill and reached the bridge Pad stopped, and leaning over the stone parapet, he pointed to a deep pool where the river emerged from a tunnel of trees.

"There!" he said, "this is my favorite place—I wanted to show you. I often swim in the pool here, it is so gloom-green and beautiful."

I liked that "gloom-green," it was just as I saw it too. We lingered there for a while, chatting easily, getting to know one another, and I liked him more each moment.

"Come on, it must be teatime; Mum will think you're not coming after all!" he exclaimed at last, breaking the spell that held us.

He seized my hand and turned me round and we raced back to the village.

The tea that was set in the sunny kitchen quite took my breath away—two kinds of bread and butter and a fruit loaf, two kinds of jam and honey, floury scones light as thistledown, three kinds of biscuits, a round of shortbread, and an enormous chocolate cake. It was a feast!

Mrs. Colquhoun was waiting to make the tea and told us to waste no time in starting on the lovely spread.

About halfway through tea Pad's father came in, smelling of paint and with a smudge of it on his cheek. He sat down next to me.

"Hello," he said, "who it this? Should I know you?"

Mrs. Colquhoun made the introductions and his intensely blue eyes twinkled at me.

"A new friend? Good, and a very paintable one," he said with a considering look. I wasn't sure what he meant but during the rest of tea I was aware of his watching me, not in an embarrassing sort of way but more . . . professionally.

Afterwards Pad and I went into his studio to see some of his pictures. There was a great variety—country, seasides, groups of people, portraits. I was tremendously impressed and Pad was pleased—he was very proud of his father.

Suddenly Mr. Colquhoun turned to me. "Elphie," he said, "next time you come I'd like to paint you— would you mind?"

I was truly delighted and felt flattered that a real artist should want to paint me.

"I would like it very much," I said, "but why me? I'm just ordinary."

"I don't think so," said Mr. Colquhoun laughing. "When can you come again—next week—Saturday?"

"Yes, come then Elphie, if you can," said Mrs. Colquhoun coming into the studio at that moment.

"Thanks, I will," I said, delighted to think that they *wanted* me to come again. "I think I'd better be going now, I've had a lovely afternoon, thank you, thank you very much."

"I'll walk back with you," Pad offered as I started off. "I want to tell you about Drisc's commission," he began, "he's much too modest to mention it himself. He has been invited to go to Australia in October to paint a mural—that's painting on a wall, you know—in one of the new churches out there. He and Mum will be away for about six months, a free trip and a whacking salary! He must be good to get a commission like that, don't you think?"

"How marvelous!" I exclaimed. "You must be very

Chapter Seventeen

proud of him. I expect he'll become famous. But what happens to you?" Surely I couldn't lose him just when I was growing fond of him?

"Well I'll be at school, of course, and in the holidays I'll go to my grandmother. Her home is only a few miles from here, and our house will be let while they're away."

Where shall I be? I wondered. Not at Barnalogie; they couldn't keep me there now that I was well again; probably I'd be stuck in some foster home miles from here, eating my heart out for Pad. The light went suddenly out of the day and I sank into a gloomy silence.

Pad noticed my dejection at once. "Cheer up!" he said, "you'll still be around, won't you?"

"That's what I don't know . . . it's not been decided yet," I murmured. "I can't stay at Barnalogie now I'm all right."

"I see," said Pad thoughtfully, "so they'll have to find a new home for you? But you like it here, this village and round about?" he asked.

"Oh I do, I *do*," I cried. "I don't want to leave here!"

We walked along in silence to the gates of Barnalogie, then Pad turned to me. "Don't worry, *we'll* see that you're all all right. Saturday then—and come early," he said.

When he had gone I loitered along the drive, reliving in my mind my happy time in Pad's home, thinking over all we had talked about. I mustn't let worries about my future dim this bright picture, so I stuffed them into the back of my mind.

I went first to tell Matron how I had got on, and came away from her office feeling quite pleased with myself, I had learned to appreciate her praise. I was surprised at my success when I thought over the afternoon. I had enjoyed talking to the Colquhouns and I had felt at ease with them as if they were old and trusted friends. It was a very different attitude from shutting myself away from everyone. What had brought about this change in me? Partly the kindness of Matron and others at Barnalogie no doubt, but most of the credit must go to Miss Ghost; through my friendship with her, my fondness for her, I had revived emotionally; *she* was the bridge between me and the rest of the world, my passport to happiness. I wondered if she *knew* how greatly she had helped me? I must see to it that she did.

That night I climbed the stairs to the turret room once again. It was dark, but an uncertain moon lit the room dimly. Miss Ada sat in her rocking chair, motionless, dejected. I dropped on my knees beside her and began to tell her about my afternoon. I told her all that had happened and how vivid those hours had been for me. At first her face was troubled, and she rocked agitatedly, but as I told my story she grew calm and still again, and in the faint moonlight I saw that she was smiling, smiling as if she were sharing my joy, as if she was happy for me.

"It's you who has helped me to make new friends," I said, "without you I might never have recovered my trust in people, my confidence in myself. Thank you, dear Miss Ada, I'll never forget you." I bent to kiss her hand, forgetting that she was without substance . . . but the chair was empty, she had vanished.

Chapter Eighteen

During the month that was left of the summer holidays I was a frequent visitor at the Colquhoun's home. Mr. Colquhoun—or Drisc, as he'd asked me to call him—had painted a head of me in which I wish I could have seen some likeness to myself, for he had given me a fugitive beauty that I would have loved to possess.

I studied the painting carefully, comparing it with the face that had once stared back at me from the bottom of the mug, the pinched face of loneliness, Miss Ada's instead of my own. Drisc saw a very different me, one that I liked much better, so what had changed me? Something in me must have begun to blossom, perhaps something to do with growing up . . . or could it be because of Pad?

Earlier in the summer a letter had come for me from Miss Black inviting me to spend a couple of weeks with her at the schoolhouse in High Stair. Matron encouraged me to go but I did not want to, I could not bear to leave Barnalogie even for a few days. I could not tear myself away from Pad and his parents for the time that was left before they would go away.

I could not even leave Miss Ada, although as the Colquhouns became more important to me, I did not need her so much, and my dependence on her lessened, my poor Miss Ghost. Soon I would have to break with her, but this would happen naturally when I left Barnalogie. If I had changed, so had she, she was no longer possessive of me, her spell over me had faded, her face was contented, serene, as if she understood her achievement and was satisfied.

The summer was nearly over, Pad would go back to school, his parents to Australia, and what would happen to me? My future was a nagging anxiety to me, so I was very glad to see Miss Jenner when she arrived unexpectedly one day and I was called into Matron's room to discuss my future. They were both pleased with me and agreed that I was a very different person from the Elspeth Harrier who had first come to Barnalogie.

"We'll miss you, Elphie," said Matron giving me a warm hug, "but it's time to move on. Where would you like to be?"

"Not with my mother in Australia!" I begged. "Don't send me there, please."

"No, no, we'll find you a nice foster home near here," said Miss Jenner soothingly. "You like this neighborhood, don't you, and Matron tells me you have made friends here."

I thought of the Colquhouns, especially of Pad—perhaps I needn't lose him after all. I think it was then that I first realized how much he meant to me, how much I cared about him—I loved him, and his parents too. And there were people in the village I was fond of, as well as Mr. and Mrs. McCann—and Matron, of course. I had regained my trust in people and had learned at last to make friends.

"Yes, I like this place and I don't want to leave it," I answered thoughtfully.

"Very well, I'll see what I can do," Miss Jenner promised, "there's no great rush." But I was not entirely reassured, it was the same old story all over again; no one really wanted me, I belonged nowhere.

Perhaps it was my unsettled state that made me think then of my father. It was a long time since I had written to him or even had news of him, and I asked Miss Jenner to find out for me how he was. Once we had been close, he and I, as Pad and his father Drisc were. Could we ever be close again I wondered? Would he ever be well enough for us to live at home together again? It was a cheerful thought . . . but only one more of my dreams.

Sometimes when I wanted a good walk outside the grounds I used to take Matron's dog Stubbs with me, and this is what I did after tea on one of the last days of Pad's holidays.

After weeks of sunshine the weather had broken, and although the rain had cleared, the ground was very wet. I put on my rubber boots and mac before the dog and I started out.

Pad had told me he was going by bicycle to spend the days with a friend in the next village, so I knew I would not see him, but I felt quite happy, for the whole of the following day Pad and I were to spend together at his home.

Stubbs and I squelched through sodden woods and took a path out on to the moor, but when it started to rain again I cut back to the road and came out at the bridge and Pad's pool. By this time there was a steady downpour again, and I was drenched and thoroughly uncomfortable.

As I crossed the bridge, I noticed a bicycle lying on the side of the road, its wheel buckled, its frame twisted as if it had skidded at the bottom of the hill and crashed into the stone wall of the bridge. A sudden awful fear froze my whole body, and I stumbled to the side of the bridge and looked over—below, on the stones by the river, a boy lay, face downwards and very still . . . it was Pad.

Chapter Nineteen

With a sickening feeling of dread I slithered down the steep bank and threw myself onto my knees beside him. I lifted his head but his eyes were shut and his face was deathly white. Blood oozed from a cut by his ear, and one of his legs was in an odd position as if it were broken. He was cold, and wet, and unconscious, and I did not know what to do. He must be badly hurt and needed help at once! I stripped off my mac and sweater, rolled the sweater into a pillow for his head, and spread my mac over him; it was pretty wet but better than nothing. Then I turned to Stubbs.

"*Stay*. Stay with him. Good dog, stay," I said and he wagged his tail as if he understood, then I scrambled up the bank and raced for the village. I blinded along through the rain and almost ran headlong into a bicycle coming in the opposite direction—Sergeant McBane the policeman. Incoherently I gasped out to him, "There's been an accident . . . Pad Colquhoun . . . he's badly hurt . . . under the bridge."

"Right, I'll see to it," he said, "here take my cape and

stay with him. Don't move him but try to keep him warm."

I nodded, I couldn't speak. He streaked off up the hill pedaling like mad towards the village, and I hurried back to Pad.

He hadn't stirred and he looked blue with cold, so I lay down beside him and spread the policeman's cape over him and Stubbs and me.

It seemed an eternity but really it was only a short time before Sergeant McBane arrived in a police car with an ambulance, followed by the doctor's car. In no time Pad, still unconscious, was in the ambulance and on his way to hospital. Dr. Cowlie went with him so I guessed he must be pretty bad.

"You and the doggy jump in with me, Elspeth, lassie, and I'll take you back to Barnalogie. You look awful wet and cold so I'll take a statement from you later," said the policeman.

"A statement? What about?" I asked, mystified.

"About the accident to young Colquhoun, lassie," Mr. McBane explained patiently. "I'll need an account of it for my records and you were the first person on the scene."

"Oh, I see . . ." I said nodding, "but I don't know what happened."

"Never mind, you found him. He might have been out there for hours if you hadn't. I was on my way to the farm and would have turned off the road before I reached the bridge. *You're* the one who probably saved his life, his parents won't know how to thank you."

It was still pouring when we reached Barnalogie, and

Sergeant McBane half carried me into the house, a be-draggled Stubbs followed. He handed me over to Matron with a brief explanation and left at once. "I'll be back later," he said.

Matron bundled me into a hot bath, then into bed, with a bowl of steaming soup to sip while she listened to my story.

"I don't know how badly hurt he is, it's a long way to fall. He must have skidded into the wall of the bridge and been thrown from his bicycle right over the top. He must be terribly injured. How soon can you ring the hospital to find out how he is . . . whether he is even alive?"

The thought of Pad dead was more than I could bear and I broke into wild sobs.

Matron put her arms round me and held me tightly. "There, my dearie," she soothed, "hush now, hush. You've been through a bad time, you're a brave girl. It's too early to ring the hospital, they won't know yet how badly the boy is hurt, but I'll ring later on, I promise. Now you tuck down and get a good night's sleep; you're worn out. Things will look better in the morning."

I was already drowsy when she left me, and in spite of my intense anxiety for Pad I must have been exhausted for I fell asleep at once. The next thing I knew it was morning and Matron was standing by my bed with a breakfast tray.

"It's good news, Elphie," she said, "your friend Pad is going to be all right. He's got a broken leg, a broken collar bone, a nasty back injury and he's badly concussed—they think no internal injuries—so he's going to be all right and perfectly fit again, though it will take some time."

Tears of relief spilled down my cheeks. "When will I be allowed to see him?" I asked.

"I don't know, dearie, we'll have to wait and see," said Matron gently. "Now eat up your breakfast, Jo-Jo is waiting to see you. I didn't let him come last night, I thought you were too tired. Come along, Jo-Jo, you can come in now," she called.

Jo-Jo sidled into the room, shy and awkward, and deposited a roll of sweets on my tray. "Bought them for you," he announced in his gruff voice.

"Oh thanks, Jo-Jo," I cried, "it's nice to see you. Were you worried about me? I'm quite OK!"

"Jo-Jo has some good news to tell you, haven't you, Jo-Jo?" said Matron.

He nodded, but he wouldn't speak, then, "Tell her," he ordered Matron.

"Mr. and Mrs. McAlister at the post office want Jo-Jo to live with them, to be his foster parents, isn't that good?" she exulted.

"Oh, I *am* glad, I'm sure you'll be happy with them," I said to Jo-Jo. But when Matron had left us, "Aren't you pleased?" I asked him. "Don't you want to go?"

He shook his head uncertainly. "You won't be there," he muttered.

"Oh Jo-Jo, you don't need *me* with you now!" I exclaimed.

But his words put an idea into my head, which I tucked away in the back of my mind.

Later in the morning when I was up and dressed,

Chapter Nineteen

Sergeant McBane came to interview me in Matron's office. He asked me a number of questions and wrote down everything I said.

"You've been very helpful," he said at the end; "this is all we're ever likely to know of what happened. It looks as if your guess is right, that he was thrown from his bicycle over the bridge—a skid probably, the roads were very wet."

"But surely Pad will be able to tell you what happened?" I suggested, "when he's better?"

Sergeant McBane shook his head. "I doubt it; he's concussed with the fall, he won't remember a thing."

I hadn't thought about the cut on Pad's head, he must have had a fearful crack on it when he landed. Supposing the crash affected his memory permanently and it didn't come back, supposing he didn't remember me, didn't even know me?

It was a horrifying thought and frightened me very much.

Presently I saw the Colquhoun's car coming up the drive and I ran down the steps to meet them.

Mrs. Colquhoun stepped out of the car and held out her arms to me, and I ran straight into them.

"He's going to be all right, Elphie . . . in time," she choked over the last words, and Mr. Colquhoun, Drisc, half lifted me off my feet with a great hug.

"When can I see him?" I asked.

"Well . . . he's conscious again. We'll ask Matron if we can take you to the hospital with us, shall we?"

"Oh yes! Yes please!" I cried.

Joyfully I led the way to Matron's office but before we went in Mr. Colquhoun stopped. "Elphie, there's something we should tell you before you see Pad," he said, "he . . . may not know you . . . his memory has not come back yet."

"I don't mind," I answered stoutly, "as long as I can see him." The seriousness of Mr. Colquhoun's words fell on my understanding like icy drops.

Matron agreed at once that I should go.

"Perhaps the sight of Elphie will jolt his memory and bring it back," she said hopefully.

"Perhaps it will, he's very fond of her . . . and so are we. It was Elphie who found him," said Pad's mother simply, putting her arm round me.

The hospital was very quiet, muffled in silence. First we saw the doctor—not our doctor—and he said we could go in to see Pad, but not to stay for long. Mr. Colquhoun stayed talking to him for a few minutes while Mrs. Colquhoun and I went into Pad's room.

His face was white and his head was bandaged, and he lay very straight and still as if it hurt him to move.

"Hullo, Mum," he said smiling dreamily. "Who is this?"

"It's Elphie—Elspeth Harrier from Barnalogie," his mother answered.

"Oh . . . hullo," he said politely—he didn't know me, there was no light of recognition in his eyes. He spoke to me as if I were a stranger he was meeting for the first time.

Chapter Twenty

So much happened in the next few weeks that I can't quite remember the order of events. The most important thing was that after a few days Pad recovered his memory. I went to see him in hospital every day, and gradually he grew stronger and more like his old self. After a couple of weeks he was allowed to go home, though he was still in plaster, and I begged to be allowed to help to look after him.

Matron agreed to let me spend part of each day at Pad's home. "It will be good nursing experience for you, Elphie," she said, "so long as you make yourself really useful."

"Of course, I will," I retorted. I intended to make myself *indispensable*.

After Pad's accident I had been too upset and worried to give much thought to Miss Ada, but once he was out of danger I began to feel rather guilty for neglecting her and decided I had better make amends. So after I got back from Pad's home one evening I went through the broom cupboard, up the little stone stair and stepped into the turret room.

I had half expected Miss Ada to be waiting for me, angry or hurt by my neglect; but the room was empty, she was not there. I must say I felt relieved, as I sat down and waited to see if anything would happen.

In a short time her chair began to rock and as I peered anxiously through the dusky room, Miss Ada herself was there. But she had become a mere shadow of herself, her form so dim, so hazy that it was only by concentrating hard that I could see her at all.

I began to explain to her what had happened. "It's my . . . friend in the village . . . Pad Colquhoun, he's had a terrible accident. I've been helping to nurse him . . . I haven't forgotten you, Miss Ada, but I've been too busy to come." She went on rocking steadily, gently, her eyes soft with understanding, with affection, her face gentle and serene, then gradually her form became more blurred, dissolving into thin air before my eyes. She had relinquished her hold on me, her task was completed, this was the end.

"Goodbye, dear Miss Ada," I said then under my breath. "Thank you, Miss Ghost."

Even as I spoke the last trace of her vanished, and only the chair was left faintly rocking. I turned and went downstairs to find Jo-Jo, whom I had also been neglecting.

I took great pleasure in helping to nurse Pad, and as he grew stronger I felt a wonderful sense of accomplishment.

"You're a born nurse," his mother told me, "have you ever thought of making nursing your career? It's a very rewarding one, Elphie."

Chapter Twenty

It was the first helpful suggestion anyone had made about my future, the thought of training to be a hospital nurse appealed to me very much.

A few days later Miss Jenner came again to give me news of my father. He was to have the brain operation of which she had once spoken, and if it was successful, he might be able to live a normal life. It would be a long time before he could leave hospital, but the possibility of his return cheered me tremendously and gave me new hope. If Miss Black asked me again to stay with her I might be allowed to visit him. At least I could write to him regularly even if he did not reply.

"There's something else I wanted to talk to you about," I told her. "I've had an idea." Just then Matron came back and sat down beside me.

"D'you think the McAlisters would have me to live with them as well as Jo-Jo, just for a few months till he settles in? He's good with me and I understand him, I could help Mrs. McAlister with him, couldn't I?"

"What a notion, Elphie!" Matron said enthusiastically. "It could work very well till Jo-Jo finds his own feet. I'll go along and see Mrs. McAlister myself."

It was all settled quite quickly, but it was not the end of surprises for me. When I went to see Pad the following day to tell him about my father, I found a family conference in progress and Pad looking positively triumphant.

"I'm coming out of plaster in a day or two," he shouted delightedly, "and there's something else . . . about you!"

"Sit down, Elphie, and listen to our plans," Drisc told me. "Pad should be able to go back to school at half-term, and we'll take off for Australia then. Has anything been settled about you?"

"I'm going to the McAlisters at the post office, along with Jo-Jo. It's to be his foster home and I'm only to be there for a short time till he gets settled." Then I went on to tell them the news of my father.

"Oh Elphie I *am* glad!" said Mrs. Colquhoun. "It's time you had some good luck. Now, we've got a suggestion to make. When you leave the McAlisters and we get home again, would you like to make your home with us here . . . till your father recovers, I mean? Pad is very keen about it, and so are we."

"Shall we make good foster parents d'you think?" asked Drisc, pulling a face at me.

"The best!" I cried. "It's too good to be true."

"So you'd like to come?" Pad broke in.

"I'd *love* to!" I said.

I went about in a dream for the rest of the day, only afraid of walking up and finding it was not real. But it *was* real, it was true, Matron reassured me about that. "They've already talked about it to Miss Jenner and me," she said. "You're a lucky girl, and you deserve it. And you'll still be around for me to keep an eye on you, Elphie," she added teasingly.

Mrs. McAlister told me more than once how glad she was that I'd be coming to them to help with Jo-Jo till the Colquhouns were home again. So it looked as if everything was going to work out well for me at last.

All too soon I had to say goodbye to Barnalogie, to Matron and the others who had cared for me.

"Come and have a good-night cup of cocoa in my room when you're ready for bed," Matron invited me on my last night in the old house, when Jo-Jo and I were all packed up and ready to move next day.

I promised to come, but first there was something I had to do.

For the last time I climbed the stair to the turret room and stepped inside. I stood in the pale moonlight relaxed and happy, conscious of the utter lifelessness of the room, it was empty, vacant, dispossessed, the rocking chair was still, Miss Ghost was gone—Miss Ghost in befriending me had released herself.

I turned my back on the turret and went down to Matron's room.

"Been saying your goodbyes, Elphie, up in that hidey-hole of yours? I've often wondered what you did with yourself all alone up there in that dismal room!"

I was so surprised I almost choked over my cocoa. Matron had known all along!

"I was never . . . quite alone," I murmured, but she had her back to me and did not hear.

"You'll come back to see us, won't you, Elphie?" Matron said when I hugged her good night.

"Of course I will," I promised.

"Maybe in the end you'll have a home of your own with your father, but in the meantime you've got a splendid chance for a happy life ahead of you—see that you make the most of it."

"Oh I will, I will," I answered.

And I thought of the new world outside Barnalogie that awaited me, first at the McAlisters with Jo-Jo to care for, then with Pad and his family, the warm, friendly circle into which he had drawn me—Pad's world—*my* world.

Author's note

I wish to thank Margery, Alison, Amy and Alistair
for the help they have given me from
their experience in working with disturbed children.